LAST MANGO IN PARIS
LARGE PRINT

MORGANA BEST

trademark, manufacturer, or otherwise, specific brand-name products and / or trade names of products.

GLOSSARY

Some Australian spellings and expressions are entirely different from US spellings and expressions. Below are just a few examples. It would take an entire book to list all the differences.

The author has used Australian spelling in this series. Here are a few examples: Mum instead of the US spelling Mom, neighbour instead of the US spelling neighbor, realise instead of the US spelling realize. It is Ms, Mr and Mrs in Australia, not Ms., Mr. and Mrs.; defence not defense; judgement not judgment; cosy and not cozy; 1930s not 1930's; offence not offense; centre not center; towards not toward; jewellery not jewelry; favour not favor; mould not mold; two storey house not two story house; practise (verb) not practice (verb); odour not odor; smelt not smelled; travelling not traveling; liquorice not licorice; cheque not check; leant not leaned; have concussion not have a concussion; anti clockwise not counterclockwise; go to hospital not go to the hospital; sceptic not skeptic; aluminium not aluminum; learnt not learned. We have fancy dress parties not costume parties. We don't say gotten. We say car crash (or accident) not car wreck. We say a herb not an herb as we produce the 'h.'

We might say (a company name) are instead of is.

The above are just a few examples.

It's not only different words; Aussies sometimes use different expressions in sentence structure. We might eat a curry not eat curry. We might say in the main street not on the main street. Someone might be going well instead of doing well. We might say without drawing breath not without drawing a breath.

These are just some of the differences.

Please note that these are not mistakes or typos, but correct, normal Aussie spelling, terms, and syntax.

AUSTRALIAN SLANG AND TERMS

Benchtops - counter tops (kitchen)
Big Smoke - a city
Blighter - infuriating or good-for-nothing person
Blimey! - an expression of surprise

Bloke - a man (usually used in nice sense, "a good bloke")

Blue (noun) - an argument ("to have a blue")

Bluestone - copper sulphate (copper sulfate in US spelling)

Bluo - a blue laundry additive, an optical brightener

Boot (car) - trunk (car)

Bonnet (car) - hood (car)

Bore - a drilled water well

Budgie smugglers (variant: budgy smugglers) - named after the Aussie native bird, the budgerigar. A slang term for brief and tight-fitting men's swimwear

Bugger! - as an expression of surprise, not a swear word

Bugger - as in "the poor bugger" - refers to an unfortunate person (not a swear word)

Bunging it on - faking something, pretending

Bush telegraph - the grapevine, the way news spreads by word of mouth in the country

Car park - parking lot

Cark it - die

Chooks - chickens

Come good - turn out okay

Copper, cop - police officer

Coot - silly or annoying person

Cream bun - a sweet bread roll with copious amounts of cream, plus jam in the centre

Crook - 1. "Go crook (on someone)" - to berate them. 2. (someone is) crook - (someone is) ill. 3. Crook (noun) - a criminal

Demister (in car) - defroster

Drongo - an idiot

Dunny - an outhouse, an outdoor toilet building, often ramshackle

Fair crack of the whip - a request to be fair, reasonable, just

Flannelette (fabric) - cotton, wool, or synthetic fabric, one side of which has a soft finish.

Flat out like a lizard drinking water - very busy

Galah - an idiot

Garbage - trash

G'day - Hello

Give a lift (to someone) - give a ride (to someone)

Goosebumps - goose pimples

Gumboots - rubber boots, wellingtons

Knickers - women's underwear

Laundry (referring to the room) - laundry room

Lamingtons - iconic Aussie cakes, square, sponge, chocolate-dipped, and coated with desiccated coconut. Some have a layer of cream and strawberry jam (= jelly in US) between the two halves.

Lift - elevator

Like a stunned mullet - very surprised

Mad as a cut snake - either insane or very angry

Mallee bull (as fit as, as mad as) - angry and/or fit, robust, super strong.

Miles - while Australians have kilometres these days, it is common to use expressions such as, "The road stretched for miles," "It was miles away."

Moleskins - woven heavy cotton fabric with suede-like finish, commonly used as working wear, or as town clothes

Mow (grass / lawn) - cut (grass / lawn)

Neenish tarts - Aussie tart. Pastry base. Filling is based on sweetened condensed milk mixture or mock cream. Some have layer of raspberry jam (jam = jelly in US). Topping is in two equal halves: icing (= frosting in US), usually chocolate on one side, and either lemon or pink or the other.

Pub - The pub at the south of a small town is often referred to as the 'bottom pub' and the pub at the north end of town, the 'top pub.' The size of a small town is often judged by the number of pubs - i.e. "It's a three pub town."

Red cattle dog - (variant: blue cattle dog usually known as a 'blue dog') - referring to the breed of Australian Cattle Dog. However, a 'red dog' is usually a red kelpie (another breed of dog)

Shoot through - leave

Shout (a drink) - to buy a drink for someone

Skull (a drink) - drink a whole drink without stopping

Stone the crows! - an expression of surprise

Takeaway (food) - Take Out (food)

Toilet - also refers to the room if it is separate from the bathroom

Torch - flashlight

Tuck in (to food) - to eat food hungrily

Ute /Utility - pickup truck

Vegemite - Australian food spread, thick, dark brown

Wardrobe - closet

Windscreen - windshield

Indigenous References

Bush tucker - food that occurs in the
Australian bush

Koori - the original inhabitants/traditional
custodians of the land of Australia in the part
of NSW in which this book is set. Murri are
the people just to the north. White European
culture often uses the term, Aboriginal
people.

1

We were sitting in the dining room at Cressida Upthorpe's boarding house. Mr Buttons had insisted on giving it a good clean to celebrate the fact that his nemesis, Dorothy, had been arrested for murder, and the silverware was sparkling. All the furnitu had been waxed and polished within an in of its life, and every piece of Victorian glassware and Victorian bone china had washed.

The conversation was lively, but that did nothing to lighten the gloomy atmosphere of the formal dining room. Two small windows afforded the only light, and the blockout eyelet curtains in various garish colours blocked most of the early morning sunlight doing its best to find its way in. Of course, it didn't help that one wall was lime green, and the other, bright red. The gloomy atmosphere was, I figured, also due to Cressida's latest painting. The huge oil on canvas took pride of place over the fireplace, and was painted in very colour imaginable, primarily red. That as, no doubt, due to the subject matter—a ant octopus eating the head of a sailor. The tomical detail was minute.

sida addressed the new boarders. "It's that you all arrived in time for ast, so we can all meet." Cressida, and ly permanent boarder, the English nan, Mr Buttons, and I had become iends in the short time that I had been in Little Tatterford, a small country town in rural New South Wales. Cressida had a penchant for applying make-up with a trowel, although she used far more finesse on her paintings. Right now she looked as though she was auditioning for the lead in a new version of the scary film, *It*.

"I don't think that French chef is really French," Mr Buttons said in a stage whisper.

Cressida looked alarmed. "Hush, Mr Buttons. He'll hear you."

I groaned and put my head in my hands. "Please don't tell me you're going to turn against every cook from now on," I whispered to Mr Buttons. The last cook had been Dorothy, a particularly unpleasant woman, and Mr Buttons had insisted she was responsible for every crime in Little Tatterford. In the end, it turned out she *was* responsible for a murder. With Dorothy in prison, Cressida had wasted no time in replacing her with Albert Dubois, a French chef direct from Paris.

"Lord Farringdon advised me to hire him," Cressida said in a tone that showed she would brook no argument. Lord Farringdon was Cressida's fat cat, and she was convinced that he spoke to her. Of course, no one had ever heard him do so. Still, it was uncanny how accurate his 'advice' had turned out to be. Cressida stood up and fetched a cat treat from the nearest walnut credenza. Lord Farringdon accepted it graciously.

Mr Buttons rolled his eyes skyward in response, and I was tempted to do the same. "Mr Buttons, you have to admit that he's better than Dorothy," I said, hoping to placate him.

"Anyone is better than Dorothy." Mr Buttons offered me a cucumber sandwich, minus its crusts.

I took one, and popped it in my mouth.

"Did you check his references thoroughly, Cressida?" Mr Buttons raised one particularly bushy eyebrow.

"Of course not," Cressida said snappily. "Lord Farringdon vouched for him. I already told you that. Besides, Dorothy had references, and she was a murderer. What good are references! Oh, here's Chef Dubois now."

The French chef appeared through the door with a flourish. "Eez ze breakfahst to zee liking?" he asked in such a thick French accent that I was hard pressed to decipher what he was saying. He was a short man, stick thin, and with a combover—as far as I could remember, as he was usually wearing a rather outsized chef's hat. He sported a particularly large handlebar moustache, and he looked like one of the line drawings from my high school French grammar book. All he needed was the French loaf of bread, a bicycle, and a spotted necktie.

"The French toast is delicious," Cressida said, and then popped half a slice in her mouth in one go.

"French toast isn't actually French," Mr Buttons whispered, more quietly this time. "It's only a slice of bread, most likely stale, soaked in egg and milk and then fried. It's not French, and he's not French, I tell you. Why, I spoke to him the other day in my perfect French, and he muttered something unintelligible in response."

"He told me he came to Australia to learn English," Cressida whispered. "Maybe that's why he doesn't want to speak French."

Mr Buttons nearly choked on his cucumber sandwich. "My dear woman, why would anyone want to come to *Australia* to learn English? That is the most preposterous thing I have ever heard."

One of the new boarders, a rather large and powerful looking man by the name of Dennis

Stanton, addressed the chef. "This food is good. What's your name again? Albert Dubois, isn't it?"

The French chef gasped and clutched his throat. "Non! It eez certainement not Al-bearh Du-bwuh! It is Al-bearh Du-bwuh!"

Dennis Stanton frowned. "That's exactly what I just said."

The chef's face turned red, so red that I thought he might have a stroke. "Non! You said, 'Al-bearh Du-bwuh,' but it eez Al-bearh Du-bwuh!" He made a strangling sound at the back of his throat.

Dennis appeared perplexed, and I was also. One of the other new boarders tried to stifle a giggle without much success. The chef left the room in a hurry. "Now, please tell me your names again," Cressida said, "and don't be upset if I get them wrong at first. We're on a first name basis here. In case you've already forgotten, I'm Cressida, and this is Mr

Buttons." Her hand flew to her throat. "Oh, Mr Buttons is the only one not to use his first name. He's English, you see." She smiled and nodded as she said it. "And this is Sibyl, who lives down the end of the lane in that little cottage. Please introduce yourselves to each other."

Dennis went first. "My name is Dennis Stanton. I lived in Sydney for years, but I'm escaping the hustle and bustle of city life and having a sea change. I'm looking around Little Tatterford for a nice house to buy."

"And my name is Wendy Mason," the woman who had tried not to laugh said. "I'm just here on a holiday, panning for gold. I've heard Little Tatterford is an old gold mining town."

I took the opportunity to study her. Wendy had an official, stern manner about her, so I had been surprised when she demonstrated a sense of humour. She was well groomed, about fifty, and seemed pleasant enough.

The last boarder appeared to be waiting for Wendy to say more, but when she didn't, he spoke. "My name is Adrian Addison. I'm in town working for the Office of Geographic Names." He spoke with an English accent, not unlike that of Mr Buttons.

I thought I had misheard him. "Excuse me," I said. "What office did you say?"

He laughed. "I know—most people haven't heard of it. I work for the Office of Geographic Names." Adrian was tall and well-dressed, possibly overdressed for a simple breakfast in a country town. He was attractive, although I wouldn't say handsome. He was covered with masses of freckles, no doubt due to his fair skin. His hair was red, but many shades lighter than Cressida's fire engine red hair. He reminded me of an older version of Inspector Humphrey Goodman, a former character from one of my favourite TV shows, *Death in Paradise*.

While I was studying him, a man burst through the door on the other side of the dining room. "I'm here!" he said loudly, scratching his stomach. His clothes were dirty and ragged.

"I can see that, my good man," Mr Buttons said. "Kindly do not make an unannounced appearance in such an uncouth state whilst others are eating."

The man ignored Mr Buttons. "Will I start work on the porch now, Cressida?"

"Yes please, Bradley," Cressida said. "When you're finished, come inside for lunch."

I noticed Mr Buttons wringing his hands in distress. Mr Buttons was somewhat of a clean freak, and clearly the man's dirty clothes were too much for him. Mr Buttons jumped to his feet, deftly pulling off his coat as he did so. He carried it over to the man and thrust it at him. "Put this on!"

The man looked shocked, but did as he asked. Mr Buttons adjusted the coat and fastened the buttons. He stood back to admire his handiwork. "Yes, that will make you far more presentable." He patted the man on the shoulder.

Mr Buttons stood aside, and I noticed that the boarders had all turned around to see what was happening.

The man looked past Mr Buttons and gasped. His eyes went wide. He clutched his throat and hurried through the door without saying another word.

2

Cressida elbowed me in the ribs. "Did you see his face?" she said in an undertone.

I nodded. "Does he know one of the boarders? He seemed alarmed at the sight of one of them."

Cressida simply shrugged. Wendy stood up and said she was going to unpack. Adrian leapt to his feet immediately afterwards. They walked out of the room, chatting. I idly wondered if they were really here to have an affair and were simply pretending they didn't know each other, but I soon dismissed that notion as fanciful. Dennis likewise yawned and stretched and then excused himself.

"The new boarders all seem nice," Cressida said, once they had left.

"What does Lord Farringdon say about them?" Mr Buttons asked rather waspishly.

Cressida appeared to think he was serious. "I haven't asked him. You see, Lord Farringdon doesn't like it when I ask him questions. He is happier simply to volunteer information to me." She nodded so hard that one of her false eyelashes fell off into her coffee.

I debated whether to mention it to her, but thought the better of it. I sipped my own coffee, after examining it for one of her false eyelashes. I wondered if all small towns were filled with eccentrics.

Cressida was still talking. "Sibyl, have you had one of your premonitions lately?"

I shook my head. "No, but I did have a weird dream last night that woke me up." I occasionally had dreams that turned out to be true, and some of them were daydreams. I hesitated to call them visions. They made me quite anxious, and I preferred not to have the ability.

"What was it about?" Cressida pressed me.

I shook my head, not wanting to go into the details. "It was just a dream about those detectives coming."

Mr Buttons cleared his throat. I looked up to see him picking crumbs from the table and forming them into a neat pile on a plate. "Which detectives, precisely? We have had more than our fair share of homicide detectives in this town. I assume they were homicide detectives?"

"Yes, Detective Roberts and Detective Henderson," I said. "The ones we didn't particularly like."

Cressida frowned. "That *is* a worry."

Mr Buttons stood up, and clutched the plate to his chest. "I'm going outside to feed these crumbs to the magpies," he said. "They have formed quite an attachment to me."

"That's because you feed them," Cressida said.

Mr Buttons did not respond, but disappeared through the door.

Cressida shrugged, and turned to me. "How are things between you and Blake?"

I beamed, unable to keep the smile off my face. Blake was my boyfriend, the town's sergeant. "Really good." I was about to say more, when I heard a loud bellow. Cressida and I looked at each other, and then ran from the dining room.

"It sounded like it was coming from out the front," Cressida said, taking off at a fast pace, with me hard on her heels.

Mr Buttons burst through the door, his face white. "He's dead!"

"Who's dead?" I asked him.

He did not respond, but pointed out the door. Cressida and I clutched each other and edged outside the house. There, lying on his back, was Bradley Brown. A thin wire was wrapped around his neck, and a mango was stuffed in his mouth.

"He might not be dead!" Cressida said. "Quick, Sibyl, ring for help!"

I immediately called an ambulance, gave them the directions, and then called Blake. "Blake, there's a dead man at the boarding house. He's been strangled, and, um, suffocated," I stammered. "He looks dead to me, but I called an ambulance just in case. Cressida is giving him mouth-to-mouth." As I spoke, she looked up at me and shook her head, but continued to administer CPR.

"Murder? Another murder?" Blake said in disbelief. The line went dead. I assumed he was already on his way to the boarding house.

"Who would want to murder a handyman?" Mr Buttons said. "He *was* rather untidy, but he didn't have a wife who would want to murder him, or any relatives that he mentioned."

I couldn't quite follow the logic of Mr Buttons' words, so I simply nodded. I could not believe there had been another murder at Little Tatterford. I took Mr Buttons' arm, and the two of us stood there, leaning over Cressida as she worked on the man.

I breathed a sigh of relief when I heard sirens in the distance. The police station was only five minutes away. Blake's police vehicle screeched to a halt outside the boarding house gate, as did one of the local fire engines. I was surprised to see it, until I remembered that the local fire fighters were trained as

Emergency First Responders. The closest ambulance was in the nearest town of Pharmidale.

The fire fighters beat Blake and Constable Andrews to the body, only just. Cressida stood aside as they examined the body.

"He's gone," one of the paramedics said after an interval.

"His mouth was full of that mango there," Cressida said, pointing to the remains of the mango. "I had to pull it out of his mouth to give him CPR."

"He was strangled," the same paramedic said, pointing to the wire around the man's neck.

Blake put his arm around me. "I'll take the three of you inside, and then I'll be back to speak to you two," he said to the paramedics. "Andrews, stay out here."

I expected Blake to take us into the living room, but he stopped just inside the door. I figured he didn't want any stray boarders going outside to the crime scene. "What happened?" Blake said simply. He pulled a notepad and pen from his jacket pocket.

"I was the one who found the body," Mr Buttons said despondently. "I was coming out to feed crumbs to the magpies, when I saw him there."

"And Cressida and I heard Mr Buttons yell, so we ran out to see what had happened," I added. "Cressida at once started CPR."

Blake patted Cressida on the shoulder. "Good work."

Cressida pulled a tissue from her pocket and wiped her eyes. "It was too late. I knew that, but I wanted to give it my best shot."

Blake made notes, and then looked up at us. "This is the new handyman, right? What's his name?"

"Bradley Brown," Cressida said simply. "He was a criminal."

Mr Buttons and I gasped. "A criminal?" Blake said. "Don't tell me he was *the* Bradley Brown, Little Tatterford's most infamous criminal, if you don't count the bushranger, Thunderbolt."

Cressida folded her arms over her chest. "Bradley hasn't been a criminal for years. He was released from prison recently. He was quite honest about it, so I thought I should give him a chance. After all, he had served his time."

"His time for what, precisely?" Mr Buttons asked through gritted teeth.

Cressida's eyes shifted from side to side. "Some sort of robbery." Her tone was defensive.

"Robbery?" Mr Buttons bellowed. "Are you quite out of your mind, my good woman?

That is most unseemly! What if he tried to rob one of us?"

Cressida made a snorting sound. "It wasn't that sort of robbery, Mr Buttons. It was an armed bank robbery. Since this is a boarding house, not a bank, we were perfectly safe." She smiled widely.

Mr Buttons and I exchanged glances. Blake rubbed his forehead. He let out one long, slow breath, and then asked, "The wire that was around his neck—has anyone seen it before?"

We all shook our heads.

"And the mango? There was a box of mangoes outside. What were they doing out there?"

"Our new French chef, straight from Paris, put them out there," Cressida explained. "They were frozen, so he put them out there to thaw. Of course, mangoes aren't in season yet, so he could only get frozen ones."

"I'd look into this so-called French chef if I were you, Blake," Mr Buttons said with a look of resolve on his face. "He's not really French. I find it strange that he turns up here, and then there's a murder."

That reminded me of something. "Blake, we were all having breakfast." I would have said more, but Blake held up his hand.

"Who is 'all'? That leads me to my next question. Who is present in the house right now? Who are the boarders?"

"Well, there's a charming man by the name of Adrian Addison," Cressida said. "There's also a woman by the name of Wendy Mason, and another man called Dennis Stanton. They all seem utterly pleasant. We only have three boarders at the moment. I hope they don't leave now that there's been a murder."

"And where are they now?" Blake asked her.

"They all arrived this morning, so they're all up in their rooms, as far as I know," Cressida said.

Blake nodded. "All right then, I'll have to question them."

I tugged on Blake's sleeve. "Bradley came into the dining room to ask Cressida if he could start work on the porch, and Mr Buttons gave him his coat."

Blake turned to Mr Buttons. "Why did you give him your coat? Was he cold?"

"I do not know whether or not he was cold, but one thing I do know is that he was dirty. I gave him my coat to cover up the worst of the filth."

Blake raised his eyebrows, but simply said to me, "Go on."

"I noticed that when he looked at the boarders, he seemed to get a fright, and he hurried out of the room."

"That's right," Cressida said. "Sibyl and I spoke about the matter at the time. His reaction was noticeable."

"And was the French chef in the room at that time?" Blake asked her.

"Yes, he was," Mr Buttons said.

I shook my head. "I don't think so. I don't think he was—are you sure, Mr Buttons?"

Mr Buttons looked perplexed. "Actually, I'm not sure. Do you remember, Cressida?"

Cressida shook her head. "No, I can't remember if he was in the room."

"All right, you three stay here and don't let anyone outside. I need to speak with the paramedics and then I'll be straight back." He waved his finger at us. "Stay here. I mean it!"

"Oh this is a dreadful state of affairs," Mr Buttons said when Blake left.

"That's for sure," I said with feeling. "It looks like one of the boarders is the murderer, and whoever it is, is staying here."

"Well, we mustn't jump to conclusions, Sibyl," Mr Buttons said. "Bradley was a bank robber, so perhaps it was one of his old gang members who came back to kill him."

"Don't forget that he looked startled to see someone in the room," I reminded him.

Before Mr Buttons could respond, Blake returned. "Constable Andrews called the detectives, and they're on their way. Right now, Andrews and I have to take statements from all of you, as well as the boarders and the French chef."

A horrible feeling settled in the pit of my stomach. "Detective Roberts and Detective Henderson, right?"

Blake nodded.

3

Cressida wrung her hands. "You don't think the police will blame Mr Buttons for the murder, do you?"

"I'm sure they won't," I said, although I wasn't sure at all. "I know he found the body, but he had only just gone outside. He didn't have time to kill anyone."

Cressida looked unconvinced. "Why do you think those horrible detectives took him down to the police station?"

"That's normal procedure, Cressida," I said.

"But they're going to question us here," she protested. Lord Farringdon came up and yowled loudly. Cressida bent down to stroke him.

"We didn't find the body. We're only witnesses after the fact, if there's any such thing. Mr Buttons was the one who actually discovered the body. Try not to worry, Cressida."

She didn't have a chance to respond, because two surly looking men entered the living room. "Well, if it isn't Sibyl Potts and Cressida Upthorpe," Detective Roberts said smugly. "This town has had so many murders, that it's a wonder anyone is left. Wouldn't you say so, Henderson?"

Detective Henderson merely nodded. I had always suspected he wasn't quite as much of a jerk as his partner.

"And it's also a wonder you have any clients at all, Ms Upthorpe, given that this boarding house has been the scene of several murders," Roberts continued.

I could feel the anger rising within me. "Have you come here to ask us questions or to make business suggestions, detective?" I said in the mildest tone I could muster.

Robert scowled at me. "All right Ms Potts, tell us what happened, right from the beginning." He held up both hands, palms outwards. "You will speak to me, and Detective Henderson will take your partner in crime into another room and question her separately."

Cressida leapt to her feet, startling Lord Farringdon. "I have not committed any crime," she said in a loud voice.

Detective Roberts ignored her. He took a seat opposite me on a rather hideous Victorian grandmother chair upholstered in a paisley design in bright hues. I knew that chair needed restuffing, so I took no small delight in seeing him shift about uncomfortably.

"From the beginning," he repeated.

"Cressida and I heard Mr Buttons scream," I began, but once more he held up both hands.

"Please relate your account from *your* perspective only, Ms Potts. You have no way of knowing what Ms Upthorpe heard, unless she told you."

His comments rankled, but I pushed on. "I was talking to Cressida, when *I* heard Mr Buttons scream. He had only left the room seconds before," I added for good measure, just in case he thought Mr Buttons had time to commit the murder. "We both raced out to the door and saw Mr Buttons running back in. He told us that Bradley, the handyman, was dead. He looked dead to me, but Cressida commenced CPR while I called emergency. And that's about it."

"Did you see anyone else outside?" He looked up from his notepad.

I shook my head. "No. I only saw me, Cressida, and Mr Buttons."

"Where were the boarders at this time?"

I shrugged. "I have no idea."

"And where were the staff?"

"There's only one staff member, a cook." I quickly amended that to, "A French chef, newly arrived from Paris. I assume he was in the kitchen."

"I'm not interested in your assumptions, Ms Potts," Roberts said with a snarl. "Facts only. It would make my job easier if you could remember that."

The French chef chose that moment to enter the room. "What has happened?" he said slowly. "There has been a murder?" His hand flew to his mouth.

"Yes," I said, and I would have said more, but Roberts moved to silence me.

"Please be quiet, Ms Potts. That will be all for now. I'm sure I'll have occasion to speak to you later. You may leave the room now and I'll question this gentleman. Your name?"

"Albert Dubois," he said timidly.

"Are you still here?" Roberts addressed me. "Close the door behind you when you leave."

I left the room, seething with anger. I pulled my phone from my pocket and texted Blake, *Roberts is a pig*. After I texted that, I was filled with remorse, because pigs are lovely animals.

Blake did not reply, so I paced up and down the long hallway and then decided to find a snack in the kitchen. The French chef was not as possessive of the kitchen as Dorothy had been, and didn't mind any of us poking around. By the time I reach the kitchen, I had lost my appetite, so wandered aimlessly back in the other direction. I walked back into the corridor and almost barrelled into Adrian Addison and Wendy Mason.

My first thought was that they looked awfully friendly with each other, but maybe I was overly suspicious. "That man, Bradley Brown, was murdered?" Wendy asked me.

The hairs stood up on the back of my neck. How did she know his name? I'm sure he had only been addressed as 'Bradley' in front of her, and she had only just arrived. Who could have told her his surname? Maybe there was a logical explanation. I looked up to see she was still waiting for my response. "Yes, I'm afraid so," I said.

She looked utterly stricken. "I think Wendy needs a brandy," Adrian said.

"Of course. There's some in the dining room." I opened the door and they both walked inside.

"Did you find the body?" Wendy asked me.

I shook my head. "No, it was Mr Buttons. He's awfully shaken up. So is Cressida; she gave him CPR. It was awful."

"Is he definitely dead?" Wendy asked me.

I nodded. "Yes."

Wendy looked stricken at the news. It seemed genuine to me—unless she was an exceptionally good actor. "Do they know who did it?" she asked me.

"I don't know," I said. "Not as far as I know, anyway. One of the detectives questioned me, and now he's questioning Albert, the chef. The other detective is questioning Cressida."

"And who is questioning Mr Buttons?" Adrian asked me. He poured a brandy from a crystal decanter sitting on top of the walnut credenza and handed it to Wendy.

"Mr Buttons has gone down to the station to give his statement," I said. "Since both detectives are here, I expect he'll be waiting at the station for quite some time." Once again, I was concerned that the detectives suspected Mr Buttons. I figured keeping him waiting was one way to make him more nervous.

Adrian nodded. "It's good to see a fellow Englishman here. How long has Mr Buttons been in the country?"

I thought it a strange question, but I figured he was trying to make conversation to take Wendy's mind off the murder. Her face was white and drawn, and she was wringing her hands nervously. "To tell you the truth, I have no idea," I said. "I haven't been in Little Tatterford for too long myself."

"Buttons is an unusual name," Adrian said. "I don't think I've met anyone else by that name."

Wendy had finished her brandy and held her glass out for another. Adrian duly refilled it. "Does Mr Buttons have any family in Australia?" Adrian asked me.

I became suspicious. These questions seemed more than idle conversation. "I don't know," I said. "You'll have to ask him. Why are you so interested in Mr Buttons?"

Adrian's eyes narrowed. "I'm sorry to pry. It's just nice to run into a fellow countryman, that's all."

It was clear to me that he was lying. But why? I had no time to puzzle over the matter because the French chef barrelled into the room in tears. "That detective, he is a buff-ohn!"

"A buff-ohn?" I asked him.

He nodded furiously. "Oui. An eed-i-ot, a clown. A buff-ohn! He asked me so many questions. Why would he think I would

murder ze man? I did not even know him!"
He burst into tears and ran into the kitchen.

I was relieved that Cressida wasn't here to see
this. She would worry that such a scene would
make the boarders leave. "I do hope you're
going to stay on," I said to Wendy and Adrian.
"The murder is nothing to do with the
boarding house. The victim was a convicted
criminal, and he did odd jobs for everyone
around town. He could have been murdered
anywhere." I nodded as I spoke, doing my
best to appear convincing.

It was Adrian's turn to look shocked. "He was
a criminal?"

I nodded. "Cressida told me he had recently
been released from prison. He was a bank
robber, so I suppose one of his criminal
associates murdered him."

"Why would they do that?" Adrian asked me.

"I don't have the slightest clue," I said honestly. "I do hope you won't leave."

"I have no intention of leaving," Adrian said with a smile. "It *is* an awful shock, but as I'm posted to Little Tatterford for work, I expect one accommodation place in a small country town is no more dangerous than another."

Wendy readily agreed. "If he was a bank robber, then clearly there isn't a serial killer on the loose," she said. "They say lightning never strikes twice in the same spot." She polished off her brandy in one gulp.

Adrian patted her shoulder.

While I was pleased that they had agreed to stay on, I was a little suspicious. If I was staying at a boarding house where someone was murdered, I would certainly hightail it out of there at the first opportunity. I suspected they had an agenda for staying here, and it wasn't the first time I had thought that.

My phone vibrated in my pocket. I pulled it out. The message was from Blake. *I agree. Are you working today? I want to call over later.*

I texted Blake back to tell him I didn't have any appointments and that I was looking forward to seeing him. In fact, I had left the week clear to catch up on paperwork. My dog grooming business was doing well, but it was hectic. I was relieved that my property settlement had finally been awarded, and even though the money had not come through yet, it was only a matter of time. I thought I should buy a house in town with the money, but I would miss Cressida and Mr Buttons if I moved from the cottage.

Still, I did not want to continue to rent a tiny one-bedroom cottage when I had the money to buy a house. And after living in Sydney, the cottage was something of a shock, being badly insulated, with holes in the floorboards, and angry possums in the roof. What's more, the chimney was always clogging up and sending smoke into the room.

Still, I had more important things to worry about. There had been a murder—another murder—in Little Tatterford.

4

Cressida and I were sitting in my cottage. I stoked the fire, trying to encourage it to burn a little better. Spring didn't mean much in this part of the world. The nights were still bitterly cold, and sometimes the days were also.

I noticed Sandy, my Labrador, eyeing a fire starter cube so I snatched it from her reach. "What is it with Labradors?" I asked her. "Why do you think everything is edible?" She stared at me and drooled.

"You're an ugly fool and a ..." I cannot repeat the rest of the sentence that came out of Max's beak. Max, my sulphur-crested cockatoo, used to be a very polite bird, until my ex-husband trained him to use foul language while he had temporary custody of him.

"Max!" I exclaimed, blushing, although I knew my admonitions would do no good.

"I'm worried that Mr Buttons has been at the police station for so long," Cressida said sadly. "I really fear the police suspect him."

I was thinking the same thing. I threw another fire starter cube on the fire. There was nothing quite so comforting as an open fire. I huddled closer, relishing the warmth, and inhaled the smoky fragrance.

A loud knock startled us both. "I didn't hear a car," I said to Cressida. I crossed to the door and opened it.

"Speak of the devil!" Max squawked. "You're a ^*$%#!"

"Max!" I said again. "Mr Buttons, come and sit by the fire."

Mr Buttons took an empty seat by the fire and held his hands towards it, rubbing them together. "It was awful, awful, I tell you. I'm quite distressed."

"I knew it," Cressida wailed. "The police think you did it, don't they?"

To my surprise, Mr Buttons shook his head. "To the contrary, my dear woman, the detectives are convinced that I was the intended victim."

I leant forward. "They are? Why?"

"Sibyl, do you have any wine?" he asked me.

I nodded. "Red or white?"

"Red, please."

I walked the few steps to my tiny kitchen and fetched an unopened bottle of wine from the cupboard. I took Mr Buttons back a glass of wine and then realised I hadn't asked Cressida if she wanted one. I did so, but she declined, so I took a seat. "Mr Buttons, you were about to tell us why the police think someone wanted to murder you."

"It's simple, my dear. He was wearing my coat."

"That seems quite tenuous to me," I said with surprise.

Mr Buttons nodded. "Yes, I think so, too. Anyone who wanted to murder me would surely know me well enough to know that I am always impeccably dressed and there is never so much as a dog hair or a piece of lint on me. Anyone who knew anything about me would not mistake me for that poor Bradley Brown. No, I myself am convinced that the poor man was surely the intended victim.

Indeed, I told the detectives that, but they merely looked at me in a supercilious fashion."

Cressida had remained silent throughout the whole exchange with her mouth open. "Sibyl, would you have any chocolate?" she asked, when she had sufficiently recovered. "I fear I'm in need of comfort food."

I walked the short five steps to my kitchen and fetched some Tim Tams from a cupboard. I tipped them onto a plate. I offered one to Cressida, but she thanked me and took the plate from me. "Don't they know he was a criminal?" she said through a mouthful of chocolate encrusted crumbs.

Mr Buttons' face lit up for the first time since he had returned from the police station. "Oh yes, they do. They told me all about him. He robbed banks."

Cressida waved one hand at him. "Yes, Mr Buttons. Don't you recall that I told you that?"

Mr Buttons shook his head. "No, you don't understand. The detectives told me all about it—in far more detail than I wanted to know, mind you. Bradley Brown was in prison for nearly fifteen years. The reason he was imprisoned for so long was that it was an armed bank robbery, but armed bank robbers usually only get short sentences."

I had been partially hypnotised by the flames, but that brought me back to the moment. "You're kidding!" I said. "I didn't know that bank robbers got short sentences."

"Please allow me to finish, ladies," Mr Buttons said, clearly exasperated. "My father always said that fools and children shouldn't see things half done. Please allow me to finish before you interrupt me again."

I nodded, and he pushed on. "When I mentioned a short sentence, I meant much shorter than fifteen years. The detectives told me that he had a gun, which is classed as robbery with a dangerous weapon. Also, he was in company which is a longer sentence."

Cressida waved a half eaten Tim Tam in front of Mr Buttons. "I know you told us not to interrupt, but you'll have to make more sense than that. In company with what?"

Mr Buttons rolled his eyes skyward. "In company with others, of course. Accomplices, if you will. Apparently, if one person robs a bank in the company of another person, each person has to serve a longer sentence than usual."

Now I really was confused. "I know you told us not to interrupt, Mr Buttons," I began, "but if I robbed a bank with you, I would get a longer sentence than if I robbed a bank alone. Is that right?"

Mr Buttons looked pleased. "Precisely. I'm glad you both understand. And robbery with a dangerous weapon, such as a gun, attracts a more severe sentence than robbery with an offensive weapon, such as a knife."

"Well, that's all very interesting," I lied, "but what does that have to do with the police thinking you were the intended victim?"

"Nothing at all," Mr Buttons said.

A piece of coal jumped from the fire and made a sizzling sound on the nearby rug. I hoped Mr Buttons wouldn't have the urge to clean it. I stomped on it with my foot, as Mr Buttons continued. "My point in telling you that was to tell you that there was a shootout with the police, and Bradley's five accomplices were killed. Bradley did not serve his full fifteen years, but got out on parole. And as we all know, he was only recently released."

"And why don't you think you were the intended victim, Mr Buttons?" I asked him.

Mr Buttons sighed. "Don't you see, Sibyl? Bradley was the only survivor of the robbery.

The gang stole just under five million dollars, and the others were killed in the shoot-out at the bank."

"So he got away with the money?" I asked him. "He wasn't arrested at the scene of the crime?"

Mr Buttons shook his head. "That's just it, Sibyl. He was arrested five weeks later. The money was never found."

I gasped, and Cressida nearly choked on a Tim Tam. "So Bradley has the money here, in Little Tatterford?" she asked him.

Mr Buttons nodded. "That stands to reason. Surely he would want the money close to him."

"But why would anyone kill him?" I said. "The murderer will never get their hands on the money now that they have killed the only person who knew where it was. Obviously, the police would've searched for it back in the day, and they never found it, so he was clever at hiding his money."

Cressida tapped her chin. "Perhaps he was killed by a relative of one of his accomplices, blaming him and wanting to take vengeance."

"Possibly," Mr Buttons said, but I could tell he was only humouring Cressida.

"He didn't seem like a rich man," I said. "He wore those old clothes."

"Think about it, Sibyl," Mr Buttons said, as he rose from his seat to wipe some chocolate from the edges of Cressida's mouth with a white linen handkerchief. "He would know the police were watching him. He would have to lie low for a while, and act as if he didn't have any money."

"Why wouldn't he grab the money and leave the country?" I asked, more to myself than to anyone else. I threw some kindling on the fire. It wasn't burning well because I had put an oversized log on it. I really needed to be more patient and start the fire more slowly, with smaller bits of wood. Thank goodness for fire starter cubes.

"Because he knew the police were watching him, like I just said." Mr Buttons smiled at me. "Most criminals aren't too bright, but he obviously had enough sense to keep cool and wait it out."

"I'm still trying to figure out who killed him," Cressida said.

Mr Buttons wrapped his arms around himself. "I hope it wasn't someone trying to kill me, after all."

I attempted to reassure him. "Who would want to murder you, Mr Buttons? That is, of course, unless you have a secret life you haven't told us about." I finished with a laugh, and looked up into Mr Buttons' face.

To my shock, he turned a pale shade of green.

5

I was about to ask Mr Buttons what was wrong, when he stood up abruptly. "I must pop out to get some more firewood."

As Mr Buttons opened the front door, Blake stepped inside. He walked straight over to me and wrapped his arms around me. I hugged him back, not caring that we had an audience.

"Get a room, you two *^%%^#!" Max squawked. "You *&^%! %$^# off!"

"Shush, Max!" everyone said in unison.

I reluctantly stepped away from Blake. "Is Detective Roberts going to give you a hard time about dating me again?"

Blake shook his head. "No, don't worry about that. You're not a suspect this time."

Mr Buttons came back with some wood and put it in the wood box. He then dusted himself down frantically, an act which caused tiny pieces of bark and dirt to fly through the air. Mr Buttons let out a shriek and ran to the bathroom. I figured he had never touched anything as dirty as firewood before. I was now even more sure that he was hiding something.

"Do they have any idea who did it?" Cressida asked Blake, offering him the last Tim Tam on the plate.

Blake thanked her but declined, and then shook his head. Mr Buttons re-entered the room, looking flustered. "Blake, do you agree with the detectives that I was the intended victim?"

Blake sat on the sofa. "No, I don't." He pulled me down next to him and put his arm around me.

Cressida nodded vigorously. "That's what Sibyl and I thought."

Mr Buttons tapped his chin. "It makes no sense. I was telling the ladies just before you arrived that if someone wanted to murder me, then they would surely not mistake me for a person as untidy as Bradley Brown."

Blake and I exchanged glances. "Mr Buttons thinks that Bradley Brown hid the millions from the bank robbery somewhere in town," I told Blake.

Blake's forehead immediately creased. "The detectives have already ordered a search of Bradley's house and the grounds, and they haven't turned up any sign of the money."

"Would he have left it in a safety deposit box, like you see on TV?" I asked him. "That's surely safer than having it in the house, say under floorboards or something. What if the house burnt down?"

Blake shook his head. "The police were looking for a key, but turned up nothing. The only keys he had were to his car and his front door. Actually, the police practically pulled his house apart looking for it. They had a team in from Sydney."

I was impressed. "That fast?"

"I suppose they looked in the roof, and behind paintings, and under the floorboards," Cressida said.

Blake smiled. "They certainly did. They looked in the chimney and in every nook and cranny. They pulled his car apart, too."

"I'd say he buried it," Mr Buttons offered. "He was a strong man, so he could have dug a deep hole."

Blake crossed his arms over his chest. "The police have been looking for that money for years and haven't turned up any sign of it. They had over a decade to look for that money. Bradley might have been expecting a raid at his own home, so he hid it somewhere else. That makes sense, anyway."

"Where else could he hide it?" I asked. "It obviously had to be somewhere where no one else would find it."

"I agree with Mr Buttons." Blake nodded in his direction. "My best guess is that he buried it."

"But I thought you said he didn't bury it at his own house?" I asked him.

Blake let out one long sigh. "This is only a guess, mind you, but I suspect he hid the money somewhere where he was working."

I thought about it for a moment. "He was working all over town, wasn't he, Cressida?" I asked her.

Cressida nodded. "He was working for me more, but he did tell me he had odd jobs all over town."

Blake leant forward. "I shouldn't be telling you this, any of it, but Roberts and Henderson checked his appointments book. He did have random odd jobs here and there, but they were all in the town itself. This was the only place he worked at that was out of town."

"And that's significant because?" My question hung in the air.

"Like I said, I'm not supposed to tell you this," Blake said, "but Roberts and Henderson think Mr Buttons is the intended victim. On the other hand, I think the murderer was someone who was after the robbery money, and as it wasn't found in

Bradley's place, I think it was buried or hidden somewhere in the grounds of the boarding house."

Cressida jumped to her feet, knocking over the plate and the one remaining Tim Tam. Somehow, I managed to grab the Tim Tam before Sandy ate it. Mr Buttons leapt up and dusted the chocolate crumbs from Cressida's bright orange jeans.

"But Blake, that doesn't make sense," I said. "Shouldn't the murderer have tortured Bradley and made him tell him where the money was? He obviously hid it very carefully, so now the murderer has no hope of finding it."

Blake held up both hands. "I don't have a clue, to be honest. I also don't have a clue why the murderer killed him in broad daylight, although I suppose it was safer to murder him out of town at a boarding house rather than murder him in town, especially if the murderer knew that everyone was inside the building."

"Still, it's quite a risk," I said.

Blake agreed. "And it's not as if the murderer was trying to make Bradley tell him and then went a little too far, because the murderer certainly would not have done that in broad daylight on the boarding house porch."

I had forgotten Cressida for a moment, but she let out a wail. "We're all in mortal danger," she said tearfully, wringing her hands.

"Please get a grip, madam," Mr Buttons said, although not unkindly. "This is no time to fall apart."

"I'm afraid Cressida is right," Blake said, his tone grim. "I do happen to think you could all be in danger. If the murderer was so brazen as to murder Bradley Brown in broad daylight and in the open, then it stands to reason that the murderer could be quite brash. It also seems to me that the murderer thought he had a good lead on the money, because surely he wouldn't have risked killing Bradley otherwise."

"And you think the money is buried at the boarding house?" Cressida said, her voice little more than a whimper.

"Buried or hidden," Blake said. "Cressida, did Bradley ever do any work inside the house?"

Cressida shook her head. "He'd come in for a cup of tea or a snack, or meals, but he was never wandering loose around the house."

"That means the money is likely hidden somewhere outside," Mr Buttons said. "Blake, he did do some repairs to the roof."

Blake's face was grim. "Look, I have to tell you that my hands are tied in this matter. Roberts and Henderson don't appear to realise any of this, because they're convinced you were the intended victim, Mr Buttons."

"What are we going to do?" I asked him.

Blake shook his head. "Nothing. Nothing at all. Sibyl, you have to promise me that you won't investigate. And that goes for all of you. Don't look for the money, and don't investigate. The murderer could quite possibly be someone at the boarding house, and if they have the slightest inkling that you're looking for the money, then your lives could be in danger. Am I making myself quite clear?"

Mr Buttons saluted; Cressida snickered, and I nodded solemnly.

Blake's eyes narrowed. "I'm still on duty, so I have to leave now. I want you all to give me your solemn word that none of you will investigate this or look for the money."

We all nodded. Blake looked at me. "Sibyl?"

I nodded again. "Sure. I won't investigate or look for the money."

Blake gave me a long penetrating look, and walked to the door.

Mr Buttons hurried after him, and then peeked behind the curtains. "Okay, he's gone. Sibyl, I expect you had your fingers crossed behind your back?"

I nodded. "Sure did!"

"I did, too," Cressida said.

"I'm sure you don't want to lie to Blake, Sibyl," Mr Buttons said, "but we have more pressing matters on our hands. Blake himself told us that Roberts and Henderson think I was the intended victim, and that means they will neglect to turn their attention to the real perpetrator of this crime. What's more, Blake told us that we could be in danger. I know he said we might only be in danger if the murderer caught us snooping, but if the money is at the boarding house, then we are in danger, anyway. We have no option but to investigate. Is everyone in agreement?"

Cressida clapped her hands. "How thrilling, another murder investigation." Her face fell. "I don't mean to sound happy, because poor Bradley is no longer here."

"I don't like lying to Blake," I said, "but I don't see that we have any other option. If those detectives were doing their duty, then we wouldn't be put in this position. If we don't find out who the murderer is, I agree that we could all be in danger."

"Sibyl, didn't you say that Bradley looked shocked when he saw one of the people in the room?"

I was about to answer, when Cressida interrupted me. "That's right! Mr Buttons, it was just after you gave him your coat. You stood aside and then the boarders were turning around looking at him. He saw one of them and gasped. Right after that, he left the room as fast as could be, as if all the hounds of hell were after him."

"And we were trying to remember if the French chef was in the room at the time," I reminded her.

Mr Buttons tapped his chin. "I think he was."

I held up my hands in a gesture of helplessness. "I really can't remember if he was."

Mr Buttons shrugged. "Nevertheless, we will have to treat him as a suspect. So that leaves us four people to investigate: the French chef, and the three boarders, Dennis Stanton, Wendy Mason, and Adrian Addison."

I agreed. "They all had the opportunity. Oh, that reminds me, Mr Buttons. Adrian was asking a lot of questions about you."

Mr Buttons' jaw dropped open, but he quickly recovered. "What did he ask, specifically?"

I tried to remember. "He asked how long you've been in the country, and he said that

Buttons is an unusual name. Oh, that's right—
he asked if you had any family in Australia."

Mr Buttons was visibly annoyed. "How rude.
What a busybody."

"I actually asked him outright why he was so
interested in you."

Mr Buttons raised his eyebrows. "And what
did he say?"

"He said it was good to meet a fellow
Englishman. You know, Mr Buttons, I think
there's more to it."

"Pish posh," Mr Buttons said dismissively.
"He's just a nosy busybody. Now, we're going
to have to investigate those four people, and
my money is on Albert Dubois. At dinner
tonight, our investigation will begin."

The rapid change of subject did not escape
my notice. Mr Buttons had a secret, and
Adrian Addison knew more about it than I
did. Whatever could it be?

6

I was sitting in the dining room, lamenting my lack of paperwork for the day. The day had been consumed with talk of our pending investigation. I didn't like keeping anything from Blake, but I really had no option.

I looked around the table at all the boarders, and shuddered at the realisation that one of them was the murderer. That is, unless it was the French chef, Albert Dubois. Wendy and Addison seemed friendly, so I wondered if they were in it together. Perhaps one of them stood watch while the other one committed the murder. And then there was Dennis. He certainly had the upper body strength to strangle someone quickly. I silently moved him to the top of my suspects list.

Chef Dubois entered the room to serve us. He looked flustered, but then again, he probably didn't have as much experience of murder as the rest of us. That is, unless he had committed the crime. He announced with a flourish that the entrée was Crevettes Sauce Boursin.

As he placed long plates with the food arranged into circles on the table, my attention was drawn by the leaves. There was one leaf on each serving, and I remembered that hemlock grew wild along the roadsides in the area. I quickly pulled my phone from my pocket and googled images of hemlock. To my relief, it did not look like the leaves on the plates.

Mr Buttons caught my eye, and I realised he wanted us to launch into our questions. Before I could do so, Wendy had one of her own. "This looks delicious," she said tentatively, "but what is it?"

The chef was visibly affronted. "I told you, it is Crevettes Sauce Boursin."

Wendy nodded. "Yes, I know that, but what's in it?"

"Prawns." The chef pointed to a large prawn sitting on top of each circle. "You not like prawns, mademoiselle?"

Wendy gave a little cough, and then said, "Is there garlic in it? I try not to eat garlic."

I bet you don't, I said to myself. She clearly had her eye on Adrian, and didn't want to laden him with garlic scented kisses. Then again, maybe I was just overly suspicious. Seeing dead bodies on a regular basis can do that to someone.

"I am also serving a wild mushroom fricassee." His voice rose to a high pitch. "It has no garlleek!"

"Did you pick those mushrooms yourself?" I piped up. I knew deadly mushrooms grew in the area, and some looked just like common mushrooms. I knew I was getting paranoid, but I prefer to be paranoid and alive rather than trusting and dead.

Chef Dubois looked at me as if I was out of my mind. "Of course not! I bought zem."

Since Mr Buttons was still staring at me and raising his eyebrows, I thought I should start the questioning. "So, Wendy, you said you're here to pan for gold?"

She nodded. "That's right."

"What creek will you be going to?"

Wendy looked alarmed. "Creek, creek?" she stammered. "Oh, I see, you're asking where

I'll be doing the gold panning. I don't know yet. Can you recommend a location?"

I thought about it for a moment. "Rifle Range Road," I said. "There's a creek at the bottom of it where most people go gold panning, just for fun. I don't know where the more serious people go."

Wendy laughed. "I'm not serious at all. I've done some gold panning out of Bathurst, at Sofala, but never in this area. I heard Little Tatterford was an old gold mining town, so I thought it would be a nice place to come to for a holiday."

Mr Buttons narrowed his eyes. "That sounds interesting. What equipment do you need for that?"

Wendy once more looked ill at ease. "Well, a gold pan. It's like a shallow piece of tin, round."

"I know what a gold pan looks like," Mr Buttons said amicably enough, "but I wondered if you needed any other equipment."

Wendy bit her lip. "No, I've only ever used a gold pan. I put water in it, shake it around, tip out the water, and see if any gold has settled in the bottom of the pan."

"Well, you'll get some gold dust at any rate," I told her. "The local farmers always say that when they dig post holes, they find lots of flecks of gold." I thought I wasn't getting anywhere with that, so I changed my approach. "So, what do you do for a living? Does it have anything to do with minerals? Are you a geologist or something?"

She shook her head. "No, it's all rather boring, actually. I work in finance."

I wondered if it would be pushing it to ask her the name of the company. While I was debating this, Mr Buttons spoke up. "And you want to move to Little Tatterford?" he asked Dennis.

Dennis nodded. "I'm retired, but I lived and worked in Sydney all my life. I got fed up with the hustle and bustle of city life, so I wanted a sea change." He laughed. "Speaking of sea changes, I can't swim. I nearly drowned as a child, so I've been wary of the ocean ever since. Plus I like cold weather, so I thought Little Tatterford would be the ideal location. Besides, the biggest house in Little Tatterford is a fraction of the value of the tiniest house in Sydney. You get so much more for your money here."

"You won't find Little Tatterford boring, after the city life?" I asked him, trying to keep the conversation going.

"Boring would be good," he said with a smile.

"You said you have retired," Mr Buttons said. "What line of work were you in?"

"That was boring, too. Now Adrian here is the one who seems to have an interesting job. Who do you work for again? The Office of Geography or something like that?"

I had to admire the way Dennis deflected the question, but I made a mental note to find out what he actually did for a living before he retired. Maybe it had some bearing on the case. At any rate, I was grateful that Blake was working tonight, because we certainly wouldn't be able to ask these questions in front of him.

Adrian smiled. "The Office of Geographical Names."

Cressida spoke up for the first time. "What do you do, exactly?"

"We are responsible for new street names. I suppose you're all aware that several new subdivisions are going up in the Little Tatterford area, and I have to approve those names."

"Surely all names would be approved automatically?" Mr Buttons asked him.

Adrian shook his head. "There was a recent famous case in Geelong, in Victoria. The developer wanted to name all the streets after *Game of Thrones* characters, but the locals objected to him naming one street *Lannister Street*. To answer your question, we have to check each street name for compliance with our rules."

"Sounds fascinating," I lied.

Adrian nodded. "We have to liaise with the council and with government bodies. I know it sounds exciting, but it's actually pretty dry work."

I looked at him to see if he was being serious about it sounding exciting, but I couldn't tell. Chef Dubois bounced into the room, holding a tray of plates. "This is Parmentier da Ratatouille," he said. "I assure you, mademoiselle, it has very little garl-leek."

Wendy smiled, despite the fact that the meal reeked of garlic. I seized the opportunity to question him. "Chef Dubois, we've all been talking about what we did before we came here. Did you come here straight from France?"

He nodded. "Yes, straight from Paris. I am here to learn the English." With that, he scurried from the room.

"Oh dear, the fire is going out." Cressida pointed, somewhat unnecessarily, to the fire. "I'll just pop outside and get some more wood. I didn't notice that the wood box was empty." There was a huge brass container in which Cressida kept the firewood for this room. I had no idea of its original use, but it looked quite impressive and imposing.

"I'll go with you," I said, not wanting to point out that she shouldn't go outside in the dark alone, not with a murderer hanging around.

We excused ourselves and walked into the kitchen, but just as I was about to open the door into the kitchen, Cressida caught my arm. She put one finger to her mouth and pointed to the door. I had no idea what she was doing until she put her ear close to the door. I did so, too, and could hear the chef speaking.

As no one was in the room with him, as far as I knew, that meant he was speaking on the phone. What's more, he was speaking in perfect English, not a trace of an accent, French or otherwise.

I couldn't make out his words, and would have listened in some more, but Cressida opened the door and marched in. I thought she was going to say something about him speaking in English, but she did not. "Chef Dubois, I'm sorry to go through your kitchen when you're preparing a meal, but we're out of firewood."

The chef put his phone on a high shelf and swung around to us. "It is of no matter. It is not good to be cold." He waved us through.

I could hardly wait to get out to the woodshed to speak to Cressida. Once we were out there, I whispered, "Did you hear him speak?"

Cressida nodded vigorously. "Yes, he was speaking English, not French, and in an Australian accent! So why is he doing that fake French accent?"

"Maybe he's the murderer," I said.

Cressida gave a little laugh. "You sound like Mr Buttons."

I had to laugh, too. "Okay, so maybe he's not the murderer, but clearly he has reasons of his own. What should we do?"

"Nothing," Cressida said with raised eyebrows. "We'll just watch him. Sibyl, are you sure you can't remember whether he was in the room when Bradley took fright?"

I shook my head. "I've been over it in my head again and again, but I can't remember one way or the other."

Cressida let out a long sigh. "Me, too," she said. "Oh well, never mind. Let's get this wood inside before we freeze to death."

After the boarders had all left the dining room and gone to their rooms, and the French chef had returned to his accommodation in Little Tatterford, we were free to speak.

"Is Blake coming over tonight?" Mr Buttons asked me.

I shook my head. "No, he had to go to Sydney for a court case. He won't be back until tomorrow at the earliest. Mr Buttons, we have information."

Cressida waved one finger at him. "And don't go jumping to any conclusions, Mr Buttons, when you hear what we have to tell you."

Mr Buttons puffed out his chest. "My good woman, I never jump to conclusions."

I spoke before he could make a long speech. "When Cressida and I went out to fetch more firewood, we overheard Chef Dubois speaking on the phone. And guess what! He was speaking in perfect English. Well, in Australian English, and not a trace of a French accent."

"He's the murderer!" Mr Buttons said with something akin to glee.

Cressida groaned. "I thought you said you weren't going to jump to conclusions."

"I'm not jumping anywhere," Mr Buttons said patiently. "I told you something was wrong with him, didn't I? And I told you both that there was something wrong with Dorothy, but you didn't believe me, did you? And now she is in prison awaiting trial for homicide. I rest my case."

"The French chef is certainly hiding something," I told him, "but we don't know just what at this point. He might not be a murderer."

"Maybe he's a thief," Cressida said cheerfully. She slipped her hand over her mouth. "No, that can't be right. Lord Farringdon vouched for him. Mr Buttons, Albert Dubois is on the straight and narrow, according to Lord Farringdon."

Mr Buttons narrowed his eyes, but did not respond. "I, too, have some news," he said.

I looked at him expectantly.

"The funeral is tomorrow."

"Tomorrow?" Cressida exclaimed. "Isn't that rather too soon?"

Mr Buttons shrugged one shoulder. "Most likely. Detective Roberts asked me to go so I could be a decoy."

"What do you mean?" I asked him.

"Remember that the police think I was the intended victim?"

"Oh." I had completely forgotten that.

Mr Buttons pressed on. "The police want me to attend the funeral to see if I can draw out the real murderer."

"Why, that is too dangerous, Mr Buttons," Cressida said, leaning over to pat his arm. Even Lord Farringdon seemed disturbed, and rubbed his chin up and down Mr Buttons' shin.

Mr Buttons pulled a tiny packet of baby wipes from his suit pocket and wiped the cat hair from his pants. "Cressida, the detectives think I was the intended victim, but we all know I wasn't."

Cressida looked embarrassed. "Silly me. All the stress is getting to me."

Mr Buttons readily agreed. "Yes, we didn't find out anything useful at dinner tonight, and one of those four people is the murderer. Blake thinks the robbery money is buried on this property somewhere. That means our lives are in danger."

7

I was sitting between Mr Buttons and
Cressida in a small wooden church building
on the southern end of town. The building
smelt musty, and I wished one of the old sash
windows could be opened to let in some fresh
air. It was cold, but not unbearably so,
although the only heating was from electric
heaters which were restricted to the vicinity
of the pulpit. Next to the pulpit was a wooden
frame with the numbers of the hymns on gold
cards, and under that was a chalkboard with

the words, *Turn or Burn!,* scrawled in big letters.

It was a dreadfully dreary church building, with the only colour being the Sunday school bulletin board to our left. The sign above a mass of pictures announced they were drawn by children under the age of six. As far as I could tell, the topic was people burning in hell. Flames seemed to be the dominant trope. "Cressida, have you been teaching art to the children of this church?"

Cressida smiled broadly. "No, but what a good idea. Maybe I should start."

"I'm so bored already," Mr Buttons said, "and it hasn't even started. Blake has had a lucky escape, being stuck in Sydney at the court hearing. I wish I'd brought a book to read."

"You shouldn't read a book during a funeral service, Mr Buttons," Cressida admonished him.

Mr Buttons' eyebrows shot skyward. "Who says so? Who made those rules?"

Cressida appeared to be at a loss. "I don't know, come to think of it. Perhaps I should have brought a book, too."

"It's good of the church to do his service for free," Mr Buttons said.

I looked at him. "I didn't know that!"

Mr Buttons nodded. "Poor Bradley Brown didn't have any relatives at all. He had zero family and zero friends. Well, maybe he made friends in prison, but they're still in there."

I thought it over. "Surely not all his friends are still in prison. He was there a long time, so many of the men who were incarcerated would have been released by now."

Mr Buttons shifted in his seat. "Maybe so, but perhaps they realised there's going to be a strong police presence here and so they didn't want to show."

"Yes, it's so good of the church to pay for his funeral and associated burial expenses," Cressida said. "This church is the only one in town that gives free funerals for people with no friends or family. It's admirable, really." She tapped her chin. "I wonder if they'll ask for hefty donations to cover the cost?"

Mr Buttons waved one hand at us both. "I think you ladies should sit over the other side of the room, just in case someone tries to kill me." He laughed. "Don't worry, I really don't think someone is after me. It's only those two bumbling detectives who think that." He nodded in the direction of the said bumbling detectives, who were standing at the side of the room.

"If they're trying to be undercover, they're not doing a very good job," I said. It was obvious to anyone that they were police officers.

Mr Buttons elbowed me in the ribs. "Why are all the boarders here, and with the French chef at that?"

Cressida stood up and waved to them. "Isn't that nice of them to come!"

"But why did they come?" I said. "Don't you think that's suspicious?"

Cressida looked taken aback. "Do you think all of them were in it together?"

I looked at the boarders and the chef. They had taken seats halfway up the church, on the right. "Actually, that hadn't occurred to me before, but I suppose it's a possibility."

"I don't trust that Adrian Addison," Mr Buttons said darkly. "He's a troublemaker and a fool."

Cressida sat back down. "Who are all these people if Bradley didn't have any friends?"

I looked around the room at the elderly ladies, all sporting fuzzy white hair and floral dresses. They all seemed to know each other, because they were chatting away happily. "I don't have a clue who they are," I said, puzzled.

"They're the churchgoers," Mr Buttons announced. "Since this church provides free funeral services for people with no friends or family, it's obvious that they'd ask their churchgoers to attend all the funerals. Otherwise, who would come? There wouldn't be anyone."

"I suppose you've got a point," I said. "That makes sense." My attention was drawn to two ominous-looking men in black suits. At first I wondered if they were detectives, but they were not interacting at all with Roberts or Henderson. "Who are those men in suits?" I asked Mr Buttons.

He followed my gaze. "They look like criminals to me. Mafia, I'd say."

Cressida readily agreed. "They're probably here to make sure Bradley is dead. Maybe he owed them money and they suspect that he faked his own death, so they've come here to make certain it's him."

"How are they going to make certain it's him?" I asked her. "They're hardly going to pop down the front and peek inside the coffin."

Cressida waved a piece of paper under my nose. "This is the notice of service, and it says that it will be an open casket."

"Isn't that a bit unusual?" Mr Buttons stopped speaking to dust the hymn book in front of him. "He was murdered, after all. Surely it should be a closed casket in those circumstances."

Cressida shrugged. "You know what these church committees are like, Mr Buttons."

He shook his head. "No, I don't. My family might have been Jacobites, but the religious tradition has not carried down to my generation."

"I didn't know your family were Jacobites," I said.

His hand flew to his mouth. "Never you mind. That was a long time ago."

"I am sure it's a matter of policy that they're all open casket," Cressida said. "There likely wasn't enough time to change the policy, given that this funeral has been pushed along."

"I have to admit, that with Roberts and Henderson staring at me so much, it's making me a little unsettled," Mr Buttons said. "They're hoping someone will leap out and attack me so they can nab him."

I sighed. "If only they would realise that Bradley was the intended victim, not you. Then they might make some inroads into solving the case."

"That will never happen," Mr Buttons began, but he could say no more as the minister took to the pulpit.

"We are here today on this very solemn occasion, to mourn the death of Bradley Brown," the minister said in a long, drawling monotone. "Mr Brown could be burning in hell at this very moment—God only knows—so I ask you all, do you know where you will spend eternity?"

I reflected that it sounded dramatic, but it certainly wasn't delivered that way. I yawned widely and wondered how long the funeral service would continue.

The minister's words were met with murmurs of approval from all the ladies in the front pews. The men in suits had taken their seat behind the church ladies, so I took the opportunity to study the three boarders and the chef. They were all sitting together, but I didn't find that in itself suspicious. To the contrary, I considered it normal behaviour for three boarders and a staff member attending the same funeral, even though it was a funeral for someone they didn't know.

I stretched again, and then saw something out of the corner of my eye. It was Constable Andrews in the opposite back row, but he wasn't in uniform. There were five other men and women sitting next to him, so I figured they were all police officers. They stuck out like sore thumbs.

The minister went on and on about hellfire and brimstone, and I grew increasingly sleepy. Mercifully, he finally stopped speaking, and told everyone to line up and pay their last respects to Bradley Brown.

"I don't want to go," I whispered. "I don't want to see him."

"You can do it, Sibyl," Mr Buttons said in an encouraging tone. "It will give us a good opportunity to watch the reactions of the boarders and the suspicious chef. Make sure we line up just after them."

"You don't have to look, dear," Cressida added. "Just pretend to. Simply avert your eyes when you get to the end of the line."

I said that I would. The three of us stood up and walked slowly over to the boarders and the chef who had shown no sign yet of standing up. I looked back at Cressida and raised my eyebrows. Mr Buttons took the matter into his own hands. "How lovely of you all to come," he said. "Please, precede us in the line."

Dennis waved one hand. "No, we'll be right."

"I insist," Mr Buttons said firmly.

Wendy stood up. "All right. Thank you, Mr Buttons." She stepped into the aisle in front of us, followed by a clearly reluctant Dennis. Adrian was the last to leave.

"I'm sure you're used to grand cathedrals rather than tiny wooden church buildings," he said to Mr Buttons with a chuckle.

Mr Buttons flushed bright red. "What was all that about?" I asked him.

"He's trying to say I'm a snob. He is being rude," Mr Buttons said in a defensive tone.

I thought there was something more to it, but I had no idea what that could be. As we drew closer to the coffin, I saw that all the church ladies appeared agitated. "It's not up to us to judge," one woman said.

Another woman nodded. "God is the only judge," she said in an overly sanctimonious tone.

"But God doesn't approve of this sort of thing," the first woman said.

All the church women nodded. "I thought this only went on in cities," one woman said, "and on TV."

"Those women are all galahs," Mr Buttons said, scratching his head.

I laughed. "Mr Buttons, you're turning Australian."

He looked alarmed. Just then, Wendy reached the end of the line. She let out a shriek. "I thought this was supposed to be a funeral for a man?"

Mr Buttons and I pushed past her. "It's a woman!" Mr Buttons said.

The minister shook his head. "That can't be right."

Mr Buttons puffed out his chest. "I assure you, sir, that I was the one who discovered the body, and I discovered the body of a man, not of a woman with blue hair and bright red lipstick, and a copious amount of pancake foundation that could sink a battleship."

The minister hurried down to the coffin. He gasped, and slammed it shut, right on the French chef's hand. The French chef let out a string of words in perfect English.

"He would swear in French if he really was French," Mr Buttons whispered.

Cressida nodded. "We've already established that he isn't French," she whispered back, "but that's not a crime."

The ladies were horrified by Chef Dubois' language, and were telling him so in no uncertain terms, several of them shaking their fingers in his face. They did not appear to care that his fingers were bleeding.

"This clearly isn't Bradley Brown," I said to the minister, trying to be helpful. "Were you doing another funeral today for this lady?"

The minister nodded. "How did this happen?"

"The funeral home has obviously delivered the wrong body," Mr Buttons said. "Can you call them and tell them?"

The minister scurried away to the pulpit. He held up his hands for silence. "Everyone, please take your seats. Mrs Whitaker, would you please come to the pulpit and lead everyone in an uplifting rendition of *What a Useless Wretch Am I*? I'll just have to make a call and get the correct coffin delivered. I want you all to stay here and sing until it arrives. It shouldn't be too long."

He turned and bolted for the side door. "I'm taking Chef Dubois home to dress his poor fingers," Cressida said. She took the unfortunate chef by the arm and led him in the direction of the door.

"I suppose I have to stay here because the detectives want someone to try to kill me," Mr Buttons said in a disgruntled tone.

"I'll stay with you," I said, none too happy. Still, I couldn't leave Mr Buttons alone.

The two of us walked back and sat in our original seats. Mrs Whitaker was singing in a dreadfully high-pitched tone, and was singing the hymn five times more slowly than it was meant to be sung. The other ladies were all singing in the same high-pitched voices, each one trying to sing over the top of the other. It sounded like a pack of dingoes down by the billabong, howling to warn of impending danger. On second thoughts, the dingoes would have been more melodious.

8

Blake had called early that morning to say he was stuck in Sydney for at least another day. While that certainly made me sad to some degree, it was nevertheless a cloud with a silver lining. Blake would take a very dim view of me investigating the murder.

I had just fed Max some birdseed and fed Sandy her breakfast, when the phone rang. "Sibyl, come up to the house immediately!"

My breath caught in my throat. "Has someone else been murdered?" I asked Cressida.

"No, nothing like that. Mr Buttons and I have realised something incredibly obvious. It's a wonder we didn't think of it before! Lord Farringdon was the one who pointed it out."

"I'll be right there."

I put on my shoes, and then had to give Sandy another treat to placate her. Every time I put on my shoes, she thought she was going for a walk. We had missed our morning walk, as it was raining.

I looked out the door, but the rain had eased somewhat. It was only a short distance to the boarding house, so I decided to walk briskly rather than take the van. Mr Buttons and Cressida were waiting on the porch for me. Cressida appeared overly animated. "Lord Farringdon told me this morning that we have missed something very obvious."

"What is it?" I prompted her.

"The murderer thinks that the bank robbery money is somewhere on the property, so the murderer is probably searching for it. *We* should search for it!" Cressida's tone was shrill.

I rubbed my forehead. "Didn't we discuss this before?" I was met with blank looks, so I wondered whether or not we had. I pushed on. "Wouldn't it be too dangerous to go looking for the money? If the murderer has even the slightest inkling that we're doing so, then we will *really* be in danger."

Cressida appeared unconcerned. "Hung for a lamb, hung for a sheep," she said blithely. "If we're in danger simply by being at the boarding house, then we might as well look for the money."

To my surprise, Mr Buttons agreed with her. He was normally the voice of reason. I shook my head. "I don't like it," I said. "If one of the boarders…"

"Or the French chef," Mr Buttons said.

"Or the French chef," I continued, "is the murderer, then how will they feel if we run around the property wielding shovels?"

Mr Buttons bit his lip. "I suppose you have a point. Why don't we think it over, while we're investigating Wendy Mason today."

"Why Wendy Mason?" I wondered why they had selected her from the others.

"Over breakfast, she said she was going gold panning out on Rifle Range Road. Cressida and I thought we should follow her to see if she really is going to pan for gold down by the creek."

"That *is* a good idea," I said, somewhat surprised.

Mr Buttons nodded. "Are you ready to go, Sibyl?"

"What, now?

"Yes. We'll go in my car, and I'll drive. We'll wait down the road, closer to town and out of sight, somewhere she'll have to drive past us, no matter which way she's going."

We had only been sitting in Mr Buttons' car on the edge of town for five minutes, and I was already getting bored. The rain had stopped; the day was heating up, and numerous blowflies were swarming through my open window. I was just about to complain, when Mr Buttons started the engine. "There she goes!"

Cressida put her hand on his arm. "Don't get too close."

I was actually impressed by Mr Buttons' tailing skills. He held back far enough to keep her from seeing him, but not so far that he would lose her. I gasped when she turned right onto the highway heading for Pharmidale.

"Perhaps she's just lost," Cressida said.

"She is heading in the opposite direction to Little Tatterford, so I'm sure she is not lost," Mr Buttons said. "Still, we shouldn't jump to conclusions. Maybe she has some shopping to do before she goes out panning for gold."

Cressida shook her head. "But remember, Mr Buttons, after she said she was going to pan for gold, we asked her if she was planning to do anything else, and she said she wasn't."

Mr Buttons shrugged. "Perhaps she simply changed her mind. Anyway, we'll follow her around Pharmidale, so long as she doesn't lose us. That is, if Pharmidale is even her destination."

The highway to Pharmidale stretched on interminably, through a vista of boring, flat ground dotted with dead and dying trees. The New England Tree Dieback was particularly bad in this part of the world. Whether the cause was bugs, pesticides, or disease, the result was an expansive tree graveyard.

The New England Highway bypassed the town of Pharmidale, and Wendy's car continued on to the town itself. "So she's going into Pharmidale itself," Mr Buttons said. "She is heading straight for the main shopping centre."

Either Wendy was lost, or she was trying to lose us, because she circled back on herself several times before heading down one of the smaller streets not far from the central shops. When she finally did pull over and parked her car, Mr Buttons parked further up the road.

I craned my neck. "Can you see what shop she's going into?" I asked him.

"I can see from here," Cressida said. "It's one of the two tourist shops in town."

"Pharmidale has *two* tourist shops?" I exclaimed in surprise. "I'm shocked it even has one. What is there to do in this town? Apart from looking at dead trees or going to the university, there is absolutely nothing else to do."

Mr Buttons and Cressida readily agreed. "I had some boarders who booked for a week to see the sights of Pharmidale," she said, "but they left the very next day. They couldn't find any sights."

I shared their opinion. "How will we find out what she's doing in the tourist shop? Should we go in there and try to find out, or should we follow her when she drives away?"

"I think we should follow her," Mr Buttons said, but Cressida disagreed.

"If we're going to ask the people at the tourist place what Wendy was doing in there, we'll have to do it soon, otherwise they won't remember who she was."

"That is true," Mr Buttons said thoughtfully, "but I think it's more important to follow her at this stage."

"Maybe we could do both," I said. "What if you follow her, Mr Buttons, and Cressida and I will go to the tourist place?"

"But how will you get back to Little Tatterford?" he asked me.

"We can catch a bus."

Cressida laughed uproariously. "Sibyl, there are only two buses between Little Tatterford and Pharmidale. One goes at six in the morning, and the other goes at nine at night."

"Let's catch a taxi then. Oh, there are taxis, aren't there?" I added, uncertain.

Mr Buttons and Cressida both nodded. "Okay, that's her now!" Mr Buttons exclaimed. "Quick, ladies, out of the car."

As soon as Cressida and I were out of the car, Mr Buttons drove off after Wendy. "What are we going to say?" I asked Cressida.

She shrugged. "Let's play it by ear."

I was dismayed. That didn't sound like much of a plan to me. Nevertheless, I followed Cressida into the shop. It was mainly filled with Indigenous artefacts in striking colours, and I wished I had time to look around. I was staring at a beautifully painted boomerang, when Cressida grabbed my arm, her bony fingers digging into my flesh. "Sibyl, look!"

There, sitting on a display table, were gold pans with several bottles of gold flakes lined up behind them. "I have an idea," I said to Cressida in low tones.

I marched over to the indifferent shop assistant. It seemed it was an effort for her to pull herself away from her phone. "Can I help you?" she drawled.

"I just missed my friend who was just in here," I said. "I saw her driving away just as I got here. I was supposed to meet her here, but I was running late. We're buying gifts for a friend of ours who has just taken up panning for gold, and we decided to buy her different gifts."

"That woman who was just in here?" she asked me.

I nodded. "What did she buy? We can't double up on the same gifts. I called her, but it's going straight to message bank."

"She bought a couple of bottles of that gold dust there," she said.

Cressida and I exchanged glances. "Thanks." I grabbed Cressida's arm, and we hurried from the shop. "I'll tell Mr Buttons, and then we'll call a taxi."

Mr Buttons spoke as soon as he answered the phone, not giving me a chance to say anything. "Stay put. I'm coming back for you. She's in a coffee shop with two other people. Cancel that taxi."

"We haven't called a taxi yet," I told him. "Who are the other people?" I looked at the phone. He had hung up.

Still, we didn't have long to wait. It was only minutes before Mr Buttons pulled up and flung the door open for Cressida, beckoning me to hurry up and get in the car.

"Who are the other people?" I asked him. I wasn't the most patient person in the world.

"The two mafia men from the funeral yesterday," he said. "Remember? The two men in the black suits."

Cressida craned her neck and looked around at me, raising her pencilled-in eyebrows. "Wow!" was all she could say.

Cressida recovered before I did. "Mr Buttons, Wendy bought bottles of gold dust from the tourist shop."

"You know, I had almost forgotten that she went into the tourist shop in all the excitement," he said. "They've picked a little remote café that no one ever goes to. Clearly, their business is not above board."

"Yes, I was watching the boarders and the French chef the whole time at the funeral yesterday," I said, "and she didn't speak to those men at all."

Cressida scratched her head. "I wonder what's going on. Mr Buttons, what can we do? They'll see us if we go inside the café."

Mr Buttons parked the car. It certainly was a remote café. In my time in Little Tatterford, I had been to most cafés in Pharmidale, but never to this one. It did not look attractive from the outside. A dirty green awning hung limply over an unpainted brick façade. There were no tables on the footpath, despite there being ample room for some. A weak breeze lifted some rubbish and blew it down the road half-heartedly.

"Perhaps one of us should go in disguise and listen to their conversation," Mr Buttons said.

"I'm not going to," I said as fast as I could, thinking it best to get in first. "Maybe you could go in drag, Mr Buttons."

"Oh well, it was a silly idea after all," he said slowly. "It's frustrating to know that they're in there talking, and we have no idea what they're saying."

I agreed. "But look on the bright side," I said. "We know she's lying about panning for gold. That was obviously her cover story for meeting these men, whoever they are. My guess is she's bought those gold flecks, so she can produce them later and say she did go gold panning."

And that's exactly what happened. The three of us had waited in the car for over an hour, until Wendy emerged. She had driven straight back to the boarding house. She did not go anywhere near the gold panning creek.

Blake was still in Sydney, so Cressida had invited me to dinner at the boarding house. "How was everyone's day?" Mr Buttons asked, coming straight to the point, the second everyone arrived.

"I've been house hunting all day," Dennis said.

"Any luck?" I asked him.

He shook his head. "Well, there were a few possibilities, but nothing that grabs me. You know how you sometimes just get that feeling when you're buying a house, and you know it's the right one for you?"

I nodded, although I had no idea. I had never bought a house. I had simply moved into my husband's house when we were married, and all my other houses had been rented.

"I've been hard at work," Adrian said. "Sadly, I'm not here on holiday."

"What about you?" Mr Buttons asked Wendy. "Did you have any luck gold panning today? You were at the creek at the end of Rifle Range Road, weren't you?"

"Yes," Wendy said with a smile. "You were right—there *is* quite a lot of gold here in Little Tatterford." She pulled one of the bottles from her pocket. I noticed she had removed the label, but she had done little else to disguise it, except add a little water. She shook it at us. "This is what I got today."

Adrian took the bottle from her and turned it over. "Wow! Is this iron pyrites—you know, fool's gold, or is it real gold?"

"Real gold," Wendy said at once, but she quickly added, "As far as I know."

Mr Buttons did a good impression of looking impressed. "That is very clever of you, Wendy. Did it take you all day to get that amount? Or just a few minutes?"

"It took me all day, unfortunately," she said, "but I think it's a good haul."

"Yes, it's quite impressive," I said dryly. I could not believe the bald-faced lies coming out of her mouth. Didn't she have a conscience? And who were the two mysterious men? I ran through all the possibilities. Could she be a hit woman, and the two men had put out a contract on Bradley? No, maybe I only thought that because I had watched the first *John Wick* the previous week. Still, I had left the room for all the gruesome scenes, which meant I hadn't seen much of the movie at all. All that aside, there was no escaping the fact that she was lying—there was no way Wendy Mason had been panning for gold that day.

9

Mr Buttons and Cressida walked me back to my cottage after dinner, given our concern that we might be in the murderer's sights. "Do you want me to check inside your cottage for you?" Mr Buttons asked me.

"Would you mind waiting here until I open the door, and if Sandy doesn't look upset, then I'll know no one's in there," I said.

Cressida laughed. "I'm sure Sandy would eat anyone who stayed still long enough. After all, she's a Labrador."

I agreed. When I opened my door, I jumped with fright. There was a body asleep on my sofa, snoring gently. I realised in a millisecond that it was Blake.

I turned around and waved to Cressida and Mr Buttons. "All clear. Thanks for walking me home." I did not want them to know that Blake was inside. I knew they would want to come in and chat with him.

Mr Buttons waved back. "Get plenty of sleep, Sibyl," Cressida said. "Don't forget I'm having another showing at the local art gallery tomorrow night."

I grimaced. Cressida's paintings amounted to nothing less than a catalogue of horrors, but they sold well despite that. They certainly weren't to my taste, but then again art is a personal thing. I, for one, preferred not to look at people being disembowelled and dismembered in glorious living technicolour, especially not when framed.

I locked the door behind me and turned my thoughts to more pleasant things—Blake. I walked over to him, noticing copious Labrador slobber all over his shoes.

I threw a soft blanket over Blake, carefully avoiding his slobber-laden shoes. The fire was dying down, so I put some more wood on it and stoked it. Blake stirred and opened one eye. "Sorry, Blake, I didn't want to wake you."

He reached out one arm and pulled me to him on the sofa. Within seconds he was spooning me, his warm arms around me. "I hope you don't mind me using my key." He nuzzled the back of my neck.

I hurried to reassure him. "Of course not. That's what it's for."

"I drove all the way back from Sydney, and I wanted to come straight to see you, but you weren't here. I realised you were up at the boarding house."

"I was. Why didn't you call?"

"I didn't want to spoil your fun. Did you get much paperwork done today?" he added.

I stopped breathing for a moment, and then realised that would make him suspicious, so forced myself to breathe normally. "Not as much as I liked." That, at least, was the truth. "How was court?"

Blake let out a long sigh. "We won in the end, but it was looking bad for a time."

"We all went to Bradley's funeral yesterday," I reminded him.

"I'd forgotten." Blake's arm tightened around me.

"The detectives were there, and Constable Andrews and other officers in plain clothes, and there were two strange men in black suits."

I was hoping Blake would comment, but he didn't. To prompt him, I added, "I wonder if the detectives are making any headway on the case."

"I know they ran a background check on the boarders."

Blake's speech was slurred, and I could tell he was falling back to sleep. "What did they find out?" I asked urgently.

Blake yawned. "I can hardly stay awake. I can't remember when I was last this tired. They found out that Dennis Stanton is a retired cop."

"A retired cop?" I echoed. "So that's his real name?"

"Yes, they're all using their real names, apart from the French chef, who isn't French by the way, but don't say I told you."

I chuckled. "We've already figured that out. Do any of them have criminal records?"

Blake's arm stiffened. "Sibyl, you're not thinking of investigating, are you?"

"Of course not." I think I might have spoken too loudly and forcefully, but Blake didn't seem to notice. "Why didn't Dennis tell us he was a cop?"

"When some cops retire, they don't want anyone to know they were cops. They just want to have a normal life."

I was thinking of more questions to ask, when I heard Blake gently snoring once more. I was perched precariously on the edge of the sofa, so I gently disentangled myself from Blake's arms. I put more wood in the fire, and placed the fireguard in front of it.

I sat on the sofa opposite Blake and rubbed my forehead. Had Bradley hidden the money on the grounds of the boarding house? It would surely make sense that he had done so here, rather than on his own property, which would be the first place people would look.

Rich basalt soil abounded in the area, so holes were easy to dig, unless someone struck rock while doing so. Of course, Bradley could have hidden the bank robbery money in one of the sheds behind the boarding house. They were so full of clutter that Mr Buttons himself wouldn't be able to clean them out. Something cleverly hidden in there could easily go unnoticed.

Cressida had not called on Bradley to do any work inside the house, and the boarding house, like most houses in Australia, had neither an attic nor a basement. That meant the money, if indeed it was on the property, was somewhere outside the boarding house.

What did we have to go on? It wasn't much. Bradley had certainly looked startled when he had seen the boarders, and I couldn't for the life of me remember whether or not Albert Dubois, whatever his real name was, had been in the room at the time. And what did I know about them? Dennis was a retired cop. Wendy pretended to go panning for gold, but instead had a secret assignation with two men, the same two men who had attended the victim's funeral, but had not spoken to Wendy throughout the service.

And what did I know about Adrian Addison? Nothing at all, apart from the fact that he was English and seemed to enjoy riling Mr Buttons. We needed to look into Adrian and Dennis more closely.

And then there was the fact that Mr Buttons seemed to have a secret of his own.

It was just then that I realised Blake hadn't answered me when I asked him if any of the suspects had a criminal record.

10

Mr Buttons and I were at the local art gallery, perusing the paintings. Not Cressida's—they were altogether too gruesome on a full stomach. We were standing in the entrance corridor, on polished concrete floors and whitewashed walls, looking at the photographs, the work of a local artist.

Cressida had come much earlier, to arrange her paintings with Mortimer Fyfe-Waring, and his friend, Vlad, or Vlad the Impaler as

Mr Buttons liked to call him. Mortimer was Cressida's agent, an art critic of note.

"I still can't believe there's a market for Cressida's paintings," Mr Buttons said in a conspiratorial tone. "It just goes to show what I know about art!"

I chuckled. "That's exactly what I was thinking."

"Is Blake coming tonight?" Mr Buttons said.

I nodded. "Yes, he was just catching up on paperwork."

"And speaking of paperwork, Sibyl, how is yours going?"

I groaned, and leant back against a piece of rough plaster between two paintings. "I was hoping to have a really productive day, but I didn't get much done. I know I should have made a list, but I didn't want to see how much I had to do, because it would frighten me.

When I'm overwhelmed with work, I get all flustered, and then I make terrible mistakes."

"You've had a lot on your mind," Mr Buttons said in a soothing tone. "We just have to get through tonight, and then we can do some more investigating tomorrow. If you have time, that is," he added. He moved aside to let some well-dressed and loud ladies past him. They were speaking in overly posh voices, the sort used for impressing their pretentious friends at such gatherings. I knew these people—they would often outbid each other for a piece of art that they did not like.

"I wonder if they actually hang Cressida's paintings after they buy them," Mr Buttons said with a laugh.

I raised my eyebrows. "You know, I'd really like to find out. She seems to be the flavour of the moment around here, and that's obviously pushing up her prices."

Mr Buttons shook his head sadly. "I really don't understand her target market. Then again, I'm no expert on art."

"You and me both," I said. "Oh look, all the boarders are here. I wonder if Albert Dubois is coming, too?"

Mr Buttons tapped his chin. He leant over to me, and said in low tones, "I would have thought the murderer would stay back at the boarding house."

"Why is that?" I asked without thinking.

"Because, Sibyl," Mr Buttons began patiently, "it would be an ideal time to look for the bank robbery money, with all of us here at the art gallery."

I slapped myself on my forehead. "Of course! It's obvious now you mention it."

"The French chef isn't here." Mr Buttons arched his eyebrows.

Cressida sailed over to us, and I did a double take. She was wearing a bright red gown. At least, I think it was a gown, because there were no other words to describe it. It appeared to have a short train, because it flowed along behind her. It was the brightest shade of crimson I had ever seen. Sugar skulls were embroidered all over it, in gleaming gold. Cressida wore matching luminescent golden blush, which she appeared to have applied to her whole face, apparently never having understood the idea of shadowing or contouring. Her lipstick was even brighter than her dress, and her eyebrows, which were always kept shaven, were drawn halfway to her hairline, giving her an expression of perpetual surprise.

I am sure I was wearing the same expression upon seeing her. I turned to see Mr Buttons coughing into one of his embroidered white linen handkerchiefs. "Are you all right, Mr Buttons?"

Instead of answering me, he turned to Cressida. "Madam, you're wearing more perfume than usual."

At first I thought Cressida looked surprised at his words, but then I realised that she couldn't look more surprised than she already did. "Oh, can you smell it? I accidentally tipped it all over my dress when I was getting ready."

"The whole bottle, obviously," Mr Buttons muttered, before sneezing violently.

Cressida ignored him. "Oh look, here's dear Mortimer with Vlad."

Mortimer sailed over, holding his hand in front of him. I wasn't sure whether he wanted me to kiss it, so I merely looked at him. He stood in front of me, his hand held out for a moment. He then took it back and seized me by my shoulders, kissing me hard on both cheeks. "Sibyl, how lovely to see you again, and Mr Buttons." He eyed Mr Buttons warily.

"You have a spot on your spectacles," Mr Buttons said to him by way of greeting. "I shall remove it for you, my good man." Before Mortimer could protest, Mr Buttons had pulled another white linen handkerchief from a pocket and scrubbed Mortimer's glasses, while Mortimer was still wearing them.

Mortimer appeared to be frozen to the spot, while Vlad was doing his best not to laugh. Vlad gave us a little wave—he wasn't one to stand on ceremony like Mortimer. When Mortimer released Mr Buttons, Cressida stepped forward and kissed him on both cheeks.

"It's lovely to see you, Mortimer. And you too, Vlad." She narrowed her eyes as she spoke to Vlad. I had often wondered whether Cressida had a crush on Mortimer. I was sure Mr Buttons thought so, not that he had ever said such a thing to me. I couldn't help but notice the way Mr Buttons acted when Mortimer was around. I had suspected for some time that Mr Buttons might have a crush on Cressida. However, my thoughts of romance turned to my own, as Blake hurried over to me.

He kissed me lightly on my cheek. "Sibyl, you look gorgeous tonight."

"So do you," I whispered back.

He took two glasses of champagne from a passing waiter, and handed one to me. "I'm so sorry we haven't seen much of each other lately."

I sipped some champagne before speaking. "That's fine. That's the life of a cop, I suppose."

He frowned and looked at me. The look spoke volumes, only I wasn't able to translate it. After an interval, he nodded. Mortimer and Cressida had already sailed away, I assume to put the hard sell on various patrons, so Blake, Mr Buttons, and I were left alone, huddled near a framed black and white photograph.

"Well, we can't stay here all night," Mr Buttons said. "Sooner or later, we shall have to sally forth and be confronted with one of those monstrosities, otherwise known as paintings by Cressida Upthorpe."

I suppressed a giggle. "Yes, we'll have to do our duty in supporting Cressida." I nodded my head ever so slightly to Wendy Mason, who was engaged in an animated conversation with Adrian Addison.

Mr Buttons at once took my meaning, and walked in their direction. I noted the clever way he stood near them, not too close to arouse suspicion, but not so far that he couldn't hear what they were saying.

I looked around for the French chef, but couldn't see him. I thought I should say something to Blake and risk a lecture about minding my business and not investigating. I took another gulp of champagne, and then said, "Do you remember how Mr Buttons always said that Dorothy was the guilty one?"

Blake laughed. I pushed on. "Now he's convinced the French chef is the murderer."

Blake raised his eyebrows. "Is it just that he's in the flow of thinking the next cook would have to be the murderer, or does he have a valid reason to be suspicious?"

I shrugged. "I have no idea, but he did note that Albert Dubois isn't here tonight. Mr Buttons thinks that the murderer would be snooping around the grounds of the boarding house, looking for the robbery money, and tonight would be a good opportunity to do it."

Blake rubbed his chin and was silent for a few moments before speaking. "Actually, that makes sense. However, Sibyl, I'm not on the case, and you're not either." He waved his finger at me as he spoke.

"Of course I'm not investigating," I lied. "Blake, don't you find it a little strange Albert isn't here when the other boarders are?"

Blake shook his head. "I don't find it suspicious at all. Perhaps he has no interest in art. I don't know why the other boarders have come, to tell you the truth. I would have thought Cressida's art wasn't to everyone's taste."

"I don't mean that," I said. "I mean, if you were the murderer and you were searching for the robbery money at the boarding house, you wouldn't come to a function when you knew that other people from the boarding house would be there, would you? You would use that opportunity to stay back and search for the money."

Blake folded his arms over his chest. "For someone who's not investigating, you seem a little too interested."

"Of course I'm interested," I said, giving him a playful punch on the arm. "I can see you don't want to talk about it, so let's go and look at Cressida's paintings."

"A cruel punishment indeed!" Blake said with a laugh.

I steered Blake in the direction of Dennis, the retired cop. He was staring at one of Cressida's paintings. It was entitled, *Entrails*. I averted my eyes, but not quickly enough. One thing was for certain—I was going to have nightmares that night. "What do you think of these paintings?" I asked him.

"Um, um," he stammered. "Well, they're not the sort of thing I would buy, but I can see the talent in them. They're so, um, realistic."

I nodded. "They're certainly not to my taste, but Cressida is a gifted artist." *If only she would use her talent for good rather than evil,* I silently added. Aloud I said, "So you won't be buying one for your new house?"

Dennis smiled. "I don't think so. I don't know enough about art to invest in it, although I have heard that art is a wise investment. I should probably stick with the stock market." He gave a rueful laugh.

"Cressida's paintings are certainly shooting up in price," I pointed out.

Mortimer must have overheard us, because he appeared at my shoulder at that point. "Yes, Cressida's paintings would certainly make a wise investment," he said.

As I made the introductions, I nearly put my foot in it by saying that Dennis was a retired police officer, a fact I wasn't supposed to know. I considered myself lucky that I caught myself just in time. Blake and I walked away, leaving Mortimer eagerly putting the hard sell on Dennis. I looked around for Mr Buttons, and spotted him still hovering around Wendy. He caught my eye and walked over to me. Adrian was nowhere to be seen. I wondered if he had doubled back to the house. If so, that was certainly suspicious.

I was about to ask Blake if he had seen Adrian, when I spotted Adrian striding towards Mr Buttons. Mr Buttons spun around, an unmistakable look of alarm on his face. "Mr Buttons, have you been in Australia long?"

Mr Buttons fidgeted. "Long enough."

"Whereabouts in England are you from?" Adrian asked him

Mr Buttons face turned bright red. "Here and there. The south."

"Whereabouts exactly?" Adrian pressed him.

"London." Mr Buttons made to move away, but Adrian stepped in front of him.

"Is Buttons your family name? That's a highly unusual name. Or is it a nickname you have given yourself?" Adrian was certainly invading Mr Buttons' personal space, and Mr Buttons was visibly uncomfortable.

"What do you want from me?" Mr Buttons asked. To me, he sounded frightened, although I couldn't see why.

"I'm writing a book and I thought you might be able to help me with my research." He was still blocking Mr Buttons' way.

"I can't help you." With that, Mr Buttons pushed past Adrian and headed for the door. I ran after him. "Mr Buttons," I said, touching his arm. "Are you all right?"

"I think I'm coming down with something, Sibyl. I have to get home. You'll go home with Blake?"

"Sure. Are you certain you're all right?"

Mr Buttons gave a short nod and hurried out the door.

I walked back to Blake. "What do you think that was about?"

Blake shrugged. "I overheard the whole exchange. It seems clear that Adrian knows something about Mr Buttons that Mr Buttons doesn't want anyone else to know." I chewed my lip, but Blake continued. "Whatever it is, Sibyl, it's none of our business. You mustn't interfere in the matter."

"It can't be anything to do with the murder, surely?"

Blake pulled me to him and kissed my head. "What do I have to do to make you forget about investigating? Sibyl, a man was murdered at the boarding house, only metres from where you live. Surely that should make you cautious."

"Oh, it does," I said in the most convincing tone I could muster. Blake continued his lecture, while my mind wandered. I would have to investigate Adrian Addison. I would start tomorrow.

Blake pulled me to him tightly. "How about we escape this place?"

I smiled widely. "Sure!"

Right on cue, Blake's phone rang. He looked at the screen and answered it at once. "Sergeant Wesley." He listened for a while, and then said, "I'll be right there."

"Emergency?" I asked him.

He smiled ruefully. "I've got to go. Sibyl, can Cressida take you home? I have to head in the opposite direction."

"That's fine."

Blake frowned. "I'm so sorry, Sibyl. I'll make it up to you." With that, he was gone. I looked after him sadly. I realised I had several hours ahead of me to look at Cressida's paintings sporting such graphic names as, *Unsuccessful Surgical Procedure*, *Impaled by a White Gum Tree Branch*, *Shark Attack*, *Eaten Alive by a Tasmanian Devil*, and my favourite, *Snakes in a Drain*.

11

Mr Buttons and I usually walked Sandy every morning, but that morning I had to walk Sandy by myself. That was the first time Mr Buttons had been a no-show. I was glad there had been a light frost, because although I didn't like the cold, it worried me to walk alone in spring and summer. Two pairs of eyes were better than one to look for snakes along the track through the bush, but it had been too cold for snakes that morning.

After taking a shower and having breakfast, I called Cressida. I didn't want to call Mr Buttons, in case he was ill and still asleep. "He didn't come down for breakfast," Cressida said. "I was concerned that he had been murdered, so I went to his room and knocked on his door. He called out that he had a migraine."

"That's not like Mr Buttons," I said, thinking back on the conversation with Adrian.

"Do you think it's to do with the conversation you overheard last night?" Cressida asked me.

I nodded, and then realised she couldn't see me. "Yes," I said. I had told Cressida all about the conversation on the way home in the car the previous night. "Cressida, do you have any free time today? I really think we should investigate Adrian Addison."

"Yes, we should," Cressida said gleefully. "Lord Farringdon says Adrian Addison is a veritable hive of information, and he's party to secrets."

I narrowed my eyes. Sometimes I really wondered about that cat.

And so, an hour later, I collected Cressida in my van. "What should we do first?" she asked me.

I fastened my seatbelt. "I think we should find out about his job for a start. Maybe he's lying about it. I think we should start with the..." I began, but Cressida interrupted me.

"Library," she pronounced.

I shook my head. "No, well yes, but I thought we should start with the Little Tatterford Council. We can go to the library later, if the council isn't any help."

The Little Tatterford Council was only about five minutes away. We easily found a park directly outside, and then walked into the gloomy building. "This is a depressing place," Cressida said. "It reminds me of silly rules, government red tape, and paying my council rates."

"I'll have to think of all that when I buy a house," I said.

Cressida gripped my arm. "I'll miss you when you buy a house, Sibyl," she said with alarm.

"Even if I buy on the other side of Little Tatterford, I won't be more than fifteen minutes away from you," I pointed out.

Cressida frowned. "But right now you're only a one minute walk from me."

I nodded. "Yes, that's the problem. I like having you and Mr Buttons so close. Anyway, there's time to think about it."

The two of us were behind a woman who was having a dispute with the man sitting behind the counter. "You've got the rates for my two properties mixed up," she said crossly. "I paid them online separately, but you've given me a credit for one house and a debit on another. Can't you ever get anything right?"

The man patiently sorted out the problem, while Cressida and I stood behind the lady. Finally, it was our turn. When the man said, "Can I help you?" I realised that I hadn't had anything planned to say.

"Um, it's like this," I stammered. "We're looking for the Office of Geographic Names."

The man leant his head to one side. "I'm sorry. The office of what? What did you say?"

"The Office of Geographic Names," I repeated. "Where would we find the office? I know they wouldn't have one in a small town like this, so is the closest one in Sydney?"

He stood up. "I'll just check for you."

He left the room, while Cressida thumbed through some pamphlets on the counter. I saw that the top one was what to do in the case of snakebite. I shuddered. He presently returned with an abrupt looking woman. "There is no Office of Geographic Names," she said quite snappily.

"Yes, there is," I argued. "I googled it."

"I was about to say that there isn't one in New South Wales. The *Office of Geographic Names* only exists in Victoria. In New South Wales, it's called the *Geographical Names Board of New South Wales*. It's under the *Geographical Names Act of 1966*, and is the statutory body for the state."

"One of my boarders, Adrian Addison, says he's working for the Office of Geographic Names," Cressida said.

"He must be from Victoria," the woman barked.

"No, he isn't," Cressida continued. "He says he's here in Little Tatterford, working for the Office of Geographic Names."

The woman snorted. "He certainly is not. Not unless you misheard the name and he's working for the Geographical Names Board. Still, there's no one from the Geographical Names Board in town at the moment, not as far as I know, anyway. Do you know anything about that, Carlton?"

The man shook his head. "No, but I can go and check." He left the room, with the woman hard on his heels.

I raised my eyebrows and turned to Cressida. "What do you make of that?"

She shrugged. "He's obviously lying. He seems the most likely murderer to me at this point."

I wasn't so sure. "I thought he and Wendy Mason might have been in it together, but whatever she's up to with those two strange men, I don't think it's linked to Adrian."

When the man returned, he shook his head. "There's no one in town from the

Geographical Names Board. I asked out back, and no one knows a thing, not even the Town Planner."

We thanked him, and left. "I knew Adrian was lying," I said to Cressida. "What's our next move?"

"The library." Cressida set off at a fast walk in the direction of the library building, which wasn't far from the council building.

"What do you think we'll find in the library?" I asked her.

"We'll google him," she said.

"We can google him at home," I pointed out. "Besides, I googled all of them—that was the first thing I did, and I couldn't find out much about any of them. Do you know how many Adrian Addisons, Wendy Masons, and Dennis Stantons there are on Facebook?"

We had reached the library door, and Cressida held it open for me. "It's clear to me that Mr

Buttons has a secret that he's hiding from us. Why he's keeping a secret from us, I cannot say. I suspect Adrian either knows Mr Buttons' secret or is suspicious about it. At least in the library, Mr Buttons can't find us searching for information on Adrian."

"You think Mr Buttons doesn't want us to investigate Adrian?" I asked her, frowning.

She nodded. "I'm certain of it. I happened to mention investigating Adrian in passing yesterday, and Mr Buttons said he was quite sure he had nothing to do with the murder. He tried to talk me out of investigating him."

I walked through the door, and at once lowered my voice. The man behind the counter looked at us. There appeared to be no one else in the library, so he was probably pleased to have patrons. When I caught his eye, he looked back down at his newspaper. "Do you think Mr Buttons was a spy, for MI6 or something like that? Perhaps Adrian was a spy too, and he's letting Mr Buttons know he's onto him."

"Mr Buttons, a spy?" Cressida whispered. "Surely not, although nothing about Mr Buttons would surprise me."

I walked over to the computers, thinking this was an exercise in futility. Cressida and I could easily google anyone on my laptop in my cottage and Mr Buttons would be none the wiser. Still, Cressida had seemed so keen on going to the library, and I didn't want to disappoint her.

The man walked over to us. He smelt overpoweringly of old cologne and cigarette smoke. "The computers are free," he said. "Are you members here?"

We both shook our heads. "The computers are free," he said again. "If you want to borrow a book, you'll have to join the library and get a library card."

"Thanks," I said, and sat at one computer, while Cressida sat at the one next to me.

"Do you want to join the library?" he said, leaning over me and displaying a full set of yellow teeth.

I leant back. "Not right now, thank you. We'll just use the computers for a little while, if that's all right."

"The computers are free," he said for what seemed to be the umpteenth time.

Thankfully, he left after that, and Cressida and I tapped away in silence for ages. "Try googling A. Addison," I whispered to Cressida. "Whatever his occupation is, he might be online with his initial only."

Cressida shook her head. "I already tried that. You were right, Sibyl. This has been a waste of time. We should leave."

I stood up, but noticed the man coming over to us. I gave him a little wave, took Cressida by the elbow, and walked as fast as I could to the front door. When we were outside, I said, "I've had an idea. Let's take a photo of Adrian and then search similar images online."

Cressida's eyebrows shot up. "You can do that?"

I nodded. "In fact, let's do it for all the suspects. And we can't discount Dennis Stanton, either. Not all police officers are above board, you know. No one is above suspicion."

"I know," Cressida said, "I'll tell them I'd like to take a photo of each of them for my records. I can pretend I'll put them in a guestbook, a happy snap for a guestbook."

"What a good idea," I said. "I think that's brilliant. And if one of them is really reluctant, then that would be suspicious. Do you think we should challenge Adrian? Tell him we know he's not working for the Office of Geographic Names?"

Cressida shook her head. "I don't think that's advisable, in case he's the murderer. He'll know we're onto him, but we don't have any evidence to have him incarcerated, so he'll be still on the loose and a threat to us. Now let's go home and cheer up Mr Buttons. Let's take him into the new pet shop in town."

I was taken aback. "There's a new pet shop in town? I had no idea. I didn't think Little Tatterford was big enough to support a pet shop."

"It's a tiny little shop," Cressida said. "It's down a side road. The only other shop near it is that little second-hand shop that's hardly ever open."

"I'm sure it won't make much money if it's not on the highway," I said.

Cressida shrugged. "I've never been in there. I just saw some nice big dog collars and leads and I thought you might like to have a look in there for Sandy. And you know how attached

Mr Buttons is to that dog—I thought that might cheer him up."

I wondered if Cressida was mistaken. They sold dog collars and leashes down at the little town supermarket, and the local hardware store sold dog food, so I found it hard to believe that there was a pet store in town. Still, stranger things had happened in Little Tatterford.

12

When we got back to the boarding house, Mr Buttons was sitting on the front steps, looking most forlorn. "All the suspects are out at the moment," he said. "The French chef who is not French is in the kitchen, however. I wanted to snoop through the sheds out the back, but I thought he might see me. If he *is* the murderer, that would put me in danger, so I've been sitting here hoping he'd leave."

Cressida reached out a hand to him. "Come with us, Mr Buttons. There's a new shop in town, and we're taking you there to cheer you up."

Mr Buttons immediately looked concerned. "What sort of shop is it?"

Cressida beamed at him. "It's a pet shop."

Mr Buttons scratched his chin. "A pet shop? Surely Little Tatterford isn't big enough to support a pet shop? After all, you can readily buy pet supplies from other stores in town."

I nodded. "That's exactly what I said. Anyway, let's have a look. It can't hurt, and we can discuss suspects on the way."

To my relief, Mr Buttons readily agreed. He certainly seemed upset by the previous night's conversation with Adrian, so I hoped the pet shop would indeed brighten his mood.

I had trouble finding a parking spot for the van directly in the vicinity of the pet shop, so I parked down the road a little way. "It's a

remote street for a shop, isn't it?" Mr Buttons
said.

"Maybe they'll go out of business soon, and
we can pick up some bargains," Cressida said
hopefully.

When we arrived at the pet shop, we stood
outside. "What a relief, it's open." Cressida
pointed to the large *Open* sign hanging on the
door, and then looked in the window. "Oh,
they seem to be only catering for big dogs.
Look at those huge collars. I suppose Great
Danes and Pig Dogs would be the only dogs
big enough to wear those collars." She leant
closer to the window. "Oh no, I was wrong.
Hmm, I've never heard of one of those dog
breeds before."

"What dog breed is that?" I asked her.

She pointed to the label. "It says *Fetish Collar*.
I wonder if a Fetish is one of those new
designer dog breeds? Or perhaps related to
the Finnish Spitz?"

I did a double take. I looked in the window at what Cressida thought were dog collars, and then the light dawned on me. "Um, Cressida," I began carefully, "this isn't a pet shop."

I shot a look at Mr Buttons, but he had turned a ghastly shade of puce green.

"Let's go in," Cressida said.

Mr Buttons held up both hands in protest. "I'm not going in there!"

Cressida was clearly most put out. She grabbed Mr Buttons by his elbow. "Mr Buttons, I'm not taking no for an answer." She all but pulled him into the shop. I could do nothing but follow them in.

"I haven't seen a pet shop like this before," Cressida said to Mr Buttons. "I'm going to buy you a gift from here to cheer you up."

Mr Buttons' jaw moved up and down, but he said nothing.

The man behind the counter smiled at her. "You're my first customers for the day. I heard you say you're looking for something for your pet?" he asked Cressida.

"I was interested in your collars," she said, "but I don't have a pet. Sibyl has a pet, and she shares her with Mr Buttons here."

The man looked surprised. "You don't say! And to think people told me that Little Tatterford was too close-minded for that sort of thing. They told me this town was too full of farmers, but you've just proven me wrong. That's good to hear. I didn't think there would be many pets in this town."

It was Cressida's turn to look surprised. "Oh no, many people in Little Tatterford have pets. Sibyl even charges to bathe the pets in town."

"You're kidding!" The man looked me up and down. "This is only a sideline, truth be told. I also fix tractors out back. I had no idea that this little town was a hotbed for such goings-on. Well, it suits me fine. It'll be great for business." He rubbed his hands together gleefully.

Mr Buttons and I clutched each other in horror. "Come on, Mr Buttons," Cressida said encouragingly. "Pick something you'd like for a gift."

"Is it your birthday?" the man asked him.

Mr Buttons shook his head. I don't think he trusted himself to speak.

"Would you like a collar for Sandy?" Cressida asked him.

Mr Buttons whimpered.

"Is Sandy your pet?" the store owner asked Mr Buttons.

Cressida answered for him. "She is really Sibyl's pet, but like I said, Sibyl shares her with Mr Buttons."

I thought Mr Buttons might pass out. Thankfully, Cressida fell silent for a moment as her attention was drawn to various items of underwear. They had a large sign, *Australiana*, emblazoned on the wall above them. "Oh how delightful," Cressida gushed. She pointed to a pair of men's underpants. Unlike the other exceptionally brief items of underwear in the shop, these were quite large, and featured a large furry koala on the front.

Cressida turned to the store owner. "Mr Buttons is English," she said, "and you know how the English just love anything that's Australian. I think I'll buy these for him. Would you like them, Mr Buttons?"

Mr Buttons finally found his voice. "Yes, please, Cressida." I expected he thought they were a lesser evil. After all, it could have been much worse. "I'm feeling a little faint. Would you mind if I waited in the car?"

Cressida waved one hand at him. "Of course not."

"I'll take him to the car," I offered quickly.

When we reached the safety of the car, I burst out laughing. "I can't believe Cressida thought that was a pet shop," I guffawed. "That's hilarious!"

"I was mortified, simply mortified," Mr Buttons said in a small voice. "I have never been in an establishment of ill repute before. Goodness gracious me, I just didn't know where to look. That will haunt me to my dying days."

I quickly suppressed my laughter. I had no idea Mr Buttons had taken it to heart. "Just as well she didn't buy you a collar or a whip," I couldn't resist saying.

Mr Buttons nodded solemnly. "I actually do like the gift that she chose in the end," he said. "It is quite an unusual novelty gift, and who doesn't like koalas! Plus they will warm one's nether regions in this cold weather."

I stared at him for a moment, wondering if he was being sarcastic. I still had not made up my mind when Cressida popped into the car and handed Mr Buttons a gift bag. He thanked her and then took out the underpants. On closer inspection, I couldn't believe my eyes. They were huge white underpants, featuring an add-on: a toy grey and white fluffy koala complete with claws and a shiny black nose.

"Do you like really like them?" Cressida said anxiously.

"Oh yes, I do, Cressida," Mr Buttons said. "I love them. Thank you."

"They're quite tasteful really," Cressida continued. "The koala neatly covers your unmentionables. It's a pity I'm not a portrait artist, or you could have posed for me in them."

"Err, yes," Mr Buttons said. He quickly stuffed the item back in its bag.

"Mr Buttons, are you going to be well enough to go for a walk today?" I asked him. "Maybe at the dog park? Blake dropped Tiny off to me this morning, but I couldn't take him for a walk with Sandy, because she leaps over him and licks him. I can't manage both dogs by myself."

"When do you want to go?" he asked me.

"How about as soon as we get back?" I said. "Then I can get stuck into some paperwork. This investigation has put me behind."

"Speaking of the investigation," Cressida said, "there's something we haven't told you yet, Mr Buttons. This morning, Sibyl and I went to the council and they told us that Adrian doesn't work for the Office of Geographic Names."

Mr Buttons' shoulders stiffened. "That's right," I said. "They said such an office doesn't even exist in New South Wales, and here it's called the Geographical Names Board. They said there's no one from that department in Little Tatterford at the moment, so clearly it's a complete fabrication."

"I suspect he's a journalist," Mr Buttons said.

"A journalist?" Cressida asked, swerving to miss a rabbit that ran across the road. "But he arrived before the murder, so why is a journalist here?"

Mr Buttons shrugged. "Your guess is as good as mine."

"What makes you think he's a journalist?" I asked him.

He shrugged again. "I can't be certain, but I have that impression."

After that, Mr Buttons clammed up. He didn't say another word all the way back to the boarding house. "I'll just make myself a cup of tea and some cucumber sandwiches and put on some warmer clothes, so could you come to the boarding house in half an hour? I'll be ready for you."

"Sure." I left Cressida and Mr Buttons at the boarding house and continued down to my cottage. Sandy and Tiny greeted me wildly. It was as if they hadn't seen me in years. "Another walk won't hurt you," I said to Sandy. "Then you'll both be tired, and I'll be able to get some work done later."

"*&^% off!" Max squawked. "You &^&%* loser! Where's your toy boy? Pretty boy. Pretty boy."

I sighed. That's what I got for leaving the window from the enclosed back area open. I opened the door to let Max out, but he just sat there on the edge of a chair, berating me. "Honestly, Max, you'd make a sailor blush," I told him. I fetched a treat and put it outside on his perch, and he flew out. I shut the door behind him and leant back on it.

I made myself a cup of coffee and sat by the remains of the fire, trying to relax. I debated whether to light the fire again, but I thought I would save the firewood and light it when I got home. Still, it was unpleasantly cold. The murderer had not struck again, so that was some consolation. Blake had told me the previous night that Detectives Roberts and Henderson were completely stumped. He said he had tried to suggest to them that Mr Buttons was not the intended victim, but they hadn't taken his words kindly. I could tell Blake was worried.

The half hour passed quickly. I popped the leashes on Sandy and Tiny, secured them in my van, and drove the short distance to the boarding house. Sandy was being her usual Labrador self, happily slobbering all over Tiny and not realising that he was getting more irritated by the minute.

Mr Buttons looked a little bit brighter when I collected him. I was burning with curiosity as to what his secret was, to be honest, although I knew it was none of my business. I just wished Adrian wouldn't upset him too much. Perhaps the walk in the fresh spring air would do him a world of good.

"Tourists," Mr Buttons said when I parked in the parking area at the dog park.

"What makes you think they're tourists?" I asked, eyeing off the group.

"They're all armed with cameras, and they're looking around," he said. "Who else would come to the dog park without dogs, and in such numbers?"

"We'll have to keep the dogs on the leashes until we're well clear of them, because Sandy will be too friendly and she might scare them."

Sure enough, two men broke away and walked over to us. "Crocodiles?" one said hopefully in a German accent. "Are there crocodiles in that creek?"

I shook my head. "No, sorry. There are no crocodiles in this state. You'll need to go up north, to Queensland."

The men looked confused.

"And if there were any in the creek, it wouldn't be safe to stand here," I continued. "Crocodiles move awfully fast on land."

The men looked upset and went back to their group. I figured they had relayed the news, as a collective sigh went up from the group.

We gave the German tourists a wide berth and set off along the track. The wide grassed area soon turned into a little bush track through gum trees. It was here that I had to watch for snakes in warm weather. "I don't think we'll need to worry about snakes today," I said to Mr Buttons. "It's still quite cold."

I pulled my scarf more tightly around my neck. To my dismay, we were not able to let the dogs off leash, because some of the tourists had wandered off to the far end of the park. I knew it wouldn't take Sandy much to knock someone over when she was trying to lick their faces in a show of exuberance.

On our way back, we came across some tourists looking up a tree. "There's a cat stuck up a tree," one of them said. "Poor kitty. She can't get down."

"Oh my goodness," Mr Buttons said. "She's right, Sibyl. There is a very large cat up that gum tree. See? Perched right in the fork. It's hard to tell because that huge bottlebrush tree is growing around the gum tree."

"I should call someone," I said.

Mr Buttons held up his hand. "No, I should be able to get it down."

I was aghast. "Mr Buttons, please tell me you're not thinking of climbing that tree?"

"I'm quite limber," Mr Buttons said smugly. "It will be no trouble. Do not worry. Leave it to me." He took off his coat and scarf and handed them to me.

When I saw Mr Buttons nimbly swing onto the lower branch of the tree, I remembered that he had been a gymnastics champion in his youth. "Be careful," I called out as he disappeared from sight, into the masses of leaves of the bottlebrush bush. I watched with trepidation as Mr Buttons emerged from a gap in the bottlebrush tree and climbed higher and higher into the gum tree. "Don't go out on one of those branches," I called out. "That's a white gum tree. They're known for dropping whole limbs for seemingly no reason."

Mr Buttons did not respond, but climbed ever higher up the tree. Finally, he reached the limb holding the cat and swung himself onto it. The tourists gasped.

Mr Buttons carefully reached out one hand for the cat. The cat apparently did not want to be rescued and hissed at Mr Buttons, lashing out at his hand. It lightly jumped past Mr Buttons and ran down the tree. The tourists clapped their hands with delight.

I heard a slight cracking sound. I knew what that meant—that sound always immediately preceded a white gum dropping a limb. "Mr Buttons!" I screamed, but too late.

13

The branch holding Mr Buttons made a further crack, a thunderous one this time, and crashed just in front of where I was standing, splintering into a thousand pieces. The tourists screamed. I held my breath as Mr Buttons fell, disappearing into the bottle brush bush. After I realised that he wasn't lying on the ground, I let out the long breath I'd been holding.

"Are you all right, Mr Buttons?" I called up into the tree, straining my eyes to see where he was.

"Yes, I'm caught up in here." His voice was faint and muffled.

I reached in my jeans pocket for my phone and realised I had left it in my van. I turned to the tourists. "Would you hurry and get your tour guide? Tell her to call for help. Tell her a man's stuck up in a tree."

Two of the tourists nodded, and took off at a run.

It was then I saw Mr Buttons' trousers caught in a sharp branch jutting out of the fallen limb on the ground. I peered once more into the tree, and this time saw Mr Buttons' naked ankles wrapped around a lower branch.

"How long can you hold on there?" I called. "I've sent for help."

"It's too far for me to jump from here," he said, worry evident in his voice.

"Here comes the tour guide now." To my relief, the tour guide was hurrying to us, accompanied by the entire group of tourists.

"What happened?" she called out before she reached me.

"Some of your tour party saw a cat up a tree, and Mr Buttons climbed up to rescue it. The cat ran off, and this branch collapsed." I pointed to the branch on the ground. "Mr Buttons is stuck in the tree. I don't have my phone on me so I couldn't call for help."

The tour guide whipped her phone from her pocket and called emergency.

"Oh look, there's a koala in the tree!" one of the tourists said with great excitement.

All the other tourists gathered around him, and pointed. "There it is," one said after the other, their cameras all clicking.

"I doubt a koala would stay around after all that commotion," the tour guide muttered after she had finished her call.

I was thinking the same thing. I turned to the tour guide. "I don't know how long he can hang on up there."

The tour guide made to respond, but the tourists were all yelling, jumping up and down, and pointing to the koala in the tree. The tour guide appeared exasperated. "There *isn't* a koala in the tree."

"Yes, there is," one said. "Look." He walked closer to the tree and pointed. "There's the koala! It's hanging upside down in that tree! Can we pat it?"

I stood directly behind the man to see where he was pointing, and then I gasped with shock. It was a koala all right, but not the sort of koala the tourists thought it was. The tour guide likewise gasped, and put her hands over the nearest tourist's eyes. "Well, I never! All of you, we must leave now!" she added in a commanding tone. She marched the protesting tourists back in the direction of the park entrance.

Thankfully, a group of fire fighters with a ladder arrived moments later. "He climbed the tree to rescue a cat, but the cat ran away and that limb broke," I told them. I pointed once more to the limb on the ground. "Can you hurry? He's hanging from the gum tree! He's caught up in that bottlebrush."

"Oh, look! There's a koala in the tree," one of the fire fighters said.

The other fire fighters peered into the tree and then burst out laughing.

"Whatever possessed you to wear those koala underpants Cressida bought you?" I asked Mr Buttons, when we were debriefing over a cup of tea and a plate of cucumber sandwiches, minus the crusts, of course.

"They were warm," Mr Buttons said in a small voice. "Sibyl, I am absolutely mortified! Absolutely mortified, I tell you." He snuffled. "Those fire fighters laughed the whole time. I hardly thought I would be disrobed by a gum tree while attempting to rescue a cat."

"And those tourists got more than they bargained for," I said, doing my best not to laugh. "I don't think the tour guide will ever look at koalas again in the same way. You might find pictures of your, um, koala, on the internet."

"It's not funny, Sibyl," Mr Buttons admonished me.

Cressida sailed into the room. She sat on one of the armchairs and poured herself a cup of tea. "You two had quite an adventure this morning, didn't you!" Her voice was altogether too cheerful, and I knew that Mr Buttons would not respond well to that.

"You could say that," Mr Buttons muttered. "I'll be scarred for life." He popped a cucumber sandwich into his mouth.

I could not resist a giggle. "So will all those tourists."

Mr Buttons glared at me by way of response. Lord Farringdon walked over, purring loudly, and stared at Mr Buttons. Mr Buttons greeted him.

"Oh well, paperwork is beckoning to me," I said, anxious to escape before Cressida informed us of Lord Farringdon's latest pronouncement. "Are we all still having coffee later in town?"

Cressida nodded, spilling some of her tea as she did so. Mr Buttons leapt up and ran from the room, presumably to get something with which to clean it. "Yes, we are," she said.

"We're not getting very far with this investigation, and I'm sure the police are no further along than we are."

"I agree, sad to say," I said. "Okay then, we'll talk about it later. Say goodbye to Mr Buttons for me."

When I walked outside, I saw Dennis Stanton sitting on the porch on the old iron seat. He greeted me. "Hello, it's a lovely day, isn't it, Sibyl?"

I agreed that it was. "How's the house hunting going?"

Dennis sighed. "I've seen a few, nothing to my liking yet. Still, houses here are so much cheaper compared with Sydney that I'll be able to afford to do a substantial renovation. I'm sure I'll find the right one soon."

"Are you only looking in Little Tatterford, or are you looking in Pharmidale, too?"

"Just in Little Tatterford," he said.

"Have you been to all the real estate agents in town?"

"Every last one," he said with another sigh. "You know, I feel quite awkward sitting here, so close to the scene of the murder. Let's walk through the rose garden."

I followed him down the steps and onto the path that ran along the front of the house. He stopped at one of the rose bushes and bent over it. "All these leaves look healthy, but there are no roses on them yet."

I laughed. "You'll have to get used to the climate here in Little Tatterford. It was a shock for me when I came from Sydney. Here, we're many weeks behind the Sydney climate. They'll have roses out in force now, but we won't get any until next month. Not many pretty flowers will grow at all in this climate. Magnolias grow well here, though, and you can get some very pretty varieties. And it's awfully hard to get fruit in season."

He nodded. "I noticed that the mangoes here haven't ripened yet, still white-green inside."

"Are you much of a gardener?"

Dennis laughed, and continued walking at a slow pace, his hands behind his back. "Not really. I like to have a nice-looking garden, but I don't want to do the work. Still, I suppose there are a few gardeners for hire around here."

"Plenty, actually," I said. "You just have to find one who knows the difference between a plant and a weed."

Dennis laughed again, only I hadn't been joking. "How many acres does Cressida have here?" he asked me.

I shrugged. "I don't have a clue, to tell you the truth. I just know she owns all this." I waved one arm expansively. "Dennis, moving from the city to a small country town takes quite a lot of adjusting. I know, because I did it not that long ago."

"What sort of adjustments?" he asked, looking at me. "Apart from the weather?"

"Well, there's the gossip," I said. An idea had occurred to me, and I wondered how I could bring it to fruition. I decided to take a risk. "For example, it's all around town that you're an ex-cop."

Dennis didn't exactly gasp, but his pace faltered. "Wow. That's quite a rumour mill you've got going here. I was hoping to be anonymous. I wonder how anyone found out?"

"You'd be surprised," I said. "Anyway, I was wondering if you could help out."

We were in the back paddock now, walking past one of the old sheds. Dennis stopped. "What do you mean?"

"I'm wondering if you could look into Wendy Mason and Adrian Addison."

Dennis frowned. "You suspect one of them murdered that man?"

I shrugged. "Well, if it wasn't me, and it wasn't you, and it wasn't Cressida or Mr Buttons, then it had to be Wendy, Adrian, or Chef Dubois. Gossip around town is that no one has a criminal record, so I was wondering if you could look into it a bit further?"

He rubbed his chin slowly. Before he had a chance to speak, I added, "And see if you can turn up anything to suggest that they were in the murder together."

"What possible motive would they have?"

I held up both hands. "I have no idea."

"Okay, I suppose I could look into it, but isn't your boyfriend a cop?"

"Yes, he is," I said dryly, "but that's why I've come to you. For one, he's not a detective, so he's not on the case, and the main reason is that he told me I can't do any investigating because it could be too dangerous."

Dennis started walking again. "He's right. Okay, I'll look into Wendy and Adrian, but yes, your boyfriend is right—it could well be dangerous. In these cases, there is usually more going on than anyone realises. Don't get involved, Sibyl."

14

Dennis's words stayed with me the rest of the day. A thunderstorm was brewing, so I didn't know if my feeling of anticipation was from the growing electricity in the air, or whether something was actually about to happen. Still, I managed to make great inroads into my paperwork, clearing most of it. Having the reward of going to a café soon certainly helped.

When I walked into the café, Cressida and Mr Buttons were already there. The café was small, and had not been decorated since the days when pale peach-pink was in fashion. A rather ghastly frieze featuring flowers in all shades of pink and red covered some of the peach-pink walls. Still, the coffee, albeit not the décor, here was good, and the pungent aroma was inviting.

Cressida waved at me frantically, but I could hardly miss her. Cressida and Mr Buttons were the only patrons in the café. I said hello to the café owner and walked over to take my seat at the table. I noted that Mr Buttons had some colour back in his cheeks, and I figured he had recovered from the koala incident. I just hoped it wouldn't turn up on YouTube.

"I'm worried that we're not investigating Albert Dubois," Mr Buttons said, raising his voice over the music playing what sounded like *Greatest Hits From the Eighties*. "It has to be him. He was planning that murder for ages."

I put my elbows on the table and rubbed my eyes. "What do you have against cooks and chefs?" I asked him. "You always said Dorothy was the murderer."

"Well, she *was* the murderer!" Mr Buttons said triumphantly.

"Dorothy committed *one* murder, but how many murders did you think she committed?" I asked him.

Mr Buttons continued to smile and nod, the logic of my words clearly lost on him. "I think it's one of the boarders," I told him. "Actually, I spoke to Dennis Stanton this morning. I asked him if he could look into Wendy and Adrian."

Cressida gasped. "But Sibyl, you've let the cat out of the bag! We weren't supposed to know he's a retired police officer!"

I hurried to reassure her. "That's fine. We were talking about what small country towns are like, and I told him there's a strong gossip mill. I did that to work into saying that I'd heard he's a retired cop."

Mr Buttons nodded approvingly. "That was clever, Sibyl."

"That's what I thought," I said with a laugh. "If I do say so myself. Of course, I'm not discounting the possibility that he *is* the murderer, but if he's not, then he might get us some useful information."

"So he agreed readily enough?" Cressida asked me.

"Yes, he did," I said. "Though he did say that it was dangerous and I shouldn't look into it too closely."

"He's right," Mr Buttons said. "Albert Dubois would be very good with knives. We know he's not French, but he's obviously a good chef, and chefs certainly know how to use knives. I'd say he strangled Bradley rather than stabbing him to throw suspicion off himself."

I rested my head on my hands. "Mr Buttons, are you completely convinced that the chef is the murderer?"

"Yes, I am," Mr Buttons said firmly. "He lied about being French."

"I'm sure everyone who has lied about being French hasn't murdered someone," Cressida said, bewildered.

The café owner came over with a tray, and set our drinks in front of us. That was one benefit of living in a small country town that I hadn't mentioned to Dennis—the staff at the cafés in town knew everyone's regular drink. There was no need to order. When she left, I said, "We know Adrian Addison lied. He isn't working for the Office of Geographic Names, or the Geographical Names Board, either. And Wendy Mason lied. She said she was going gold panning, but she didn't, and she met with those two men. Wendy and Adrian are acting far more suspiciously than the chef."

"Just because we don't know what lies Albert Dubois has told us, doesn't mean he's not lying," Mr Buttons pointed out.

My head was spinning, so I sipped my half strength latte on almond milk. The caffeine made me feel a little better and kicked my synapses into gear. "I just feel we're going around in circles," I lamented. "We have four suspects, and we really don't know anything about them."

One of the local real estate agents walked in and ordered. She popped over to our table to say hello. "Will you join us?" Cressida said.

She shook her head. "I'm just popping in for a quick coffee between appointments. I'm grabbing some coffee to take back to my office."

"How's business?" Cressida asked her.

"Slow," she said sadly. "There are more listings than buyers. I've shown several people around the last week, and they've looked at everything I have on my books and haven't been interested in a single one."

I nodded. "Oh yes, one of Cressida's boarders, Dennis Stanton, was looking."

"Tell him to come and see me," she said.

"Hasn't he been already?" I asked her. "He told me he had been to every real estate agent in town."

She looked puzzled. "What did you say his name was again?"

"Dennis Stanton."

She shook her head. "No, I haven't shown anyone by that name any listings."

The café owner called her away at that point and handed her coffee to her. After she left, I said, "Okay, now that's suspicious. When I asked Dennis if he had been to all the real estate agents in town, he said that he had."

Mr Buttons tapped his chin. "Yes and she's one of the two bigger real estate agents in town, so he surely would have been to her, what with her office on the highway and everything."

"We googled him at length, didn't we?" I said, trying to remember.

Cressida and Mr Buttons both nodded. "There were millions of Dennis Stantons, though, remember?" Cressida added. "We didn't find anything about him, or the others, for that matter."

"What if Dennis really isn't here looking for a house to buy?" I said. "We need to find out. Cressida, do you know any of the other real estate agents in town?"

"Of course I do," she said. "I know all of them."

"Who would be the main one," I asked her, "apart from the lady who was just in here."

"That's easy," Cressida said. "It's the office just down from here."

"Cressida, after you drink your coffee, could you pop in and ask them if Dennis Stanton has been viewing properties with them and if he's made any enquiries at all?"

Cressida downed the rest of her coffee in one gulp. "Sure, I'll go right now."

"She left before she could order cake," Mr Buttons said sadly. "Perhaps we shouldn't order cake until she comes back."

"Why don't we just order her usual," I said, "and if she doesn't like it, you can eat hers and she can order something else."

Mr Buttons' face lit up. "What a great idea, Sibyl."

By the time Cressida got back, her blueberry cheesecake was on the table. "We ordered for you," Mr Buttons said. "If you don't want it, we can swap it for something else."

Cressida had already eaten some of it before he had finished speaking. "No, this is what I wanted," she said. "You won't believe this. That office had never heard of him."

"They were sure?" I asked.

She nodded. "Yes, so Dennis Stanton is here under a pretext."

"Whatever could it be?" I said. "Do you think Dennis is the murderer?" Mr Buttons and Cressida both shrugged, and I sighed. "Each one of our suspects has a secret," I said. "That certainly isn't helping us narrow it down at all."

Cressida and Mr Buttons did not respond—
they were too busy eating their cakes. I gave
up and did likewise. I was frustrated that we
didn't have a good lead on the suspects. The
more we investigated, the more puzzling it all
became. To make matters worse, I was sure
the detectives didn't even know as much as
we did.

I was wondering whether to order some more
coffee, when a thought occurred to me.
"There's something we haven't investigated!" I
said excitedly.

Cressida and Mr Buttons looked up, their
cake forks halfway to their mouths.

"We haven't investigated Bradley Brown."

Mr Buttons swallowed hard, and then said,
"But he's dead!"

I shook my head. "Don't you see! We need to
google him."

"We already have," he protested.

"No, we haven't," I pointed out. "We only googled the gang, and their robberies. We really need to research him in depth."

Mr Buttons pulled a face. "I'm not sure where you're going with this."

"Well then, here's an example. Let's just say that we googled him and found out he had a sister. Maybe their father died and left him everything in the will, and nothing for the sister. Maybe his sister is Wendy Mason, and she murdered him to inherit the money."

"But they looked nothing alike," Cressida protested. "I'm sure they're not related."

I took a deep breath before speaking. "I just made that up off the top of my head, Cressida," I said patiently. "It's completely hypothetical. I'm just saying that if we google him, we might uncover some information that will lead to us discovering who murdered him."

Mr Buttons smiled. "Sibyl, that's the best idea you've had all day."

A short time later, we were sitting in the private living room at the boarding house. Smaller than the main living room, the private room had even more antiques, if that could be believed. Unfortunately, Cressida had recently redecorated it, and for an artist, she sure had weird taste in paint colours for interior walls. One wall was bright blue and the opposite wall was metallic gold. Cressida had painted the other two walls in a marble effect. Consequently, the marble walls always made me feel as if I were in a horror movie, the walls closing in on me.

As usual, the faint smell of mould hung on the air. This was the least ventilated room in the old house. "Cressida," I said, "would you like me to fill the diffuser I bought you?"

Cressida leant to one side and switched on said gift. "Oh, Sibyl, I completely forgot to turn it on. I filled it this morning with water and essential oil just like you showed me. I just can't remember which oil I used."

"Vetiver," I said, when the bitter smell wafted out. "Hmm, you didn't like that lavender oil I bought you?"

Cressida smiled widely. "Oh, I did, Sibyl, thank you. I read somewhere that vetiver was a perfume ingredient and so I thought it would be nice to try it."

Mr Buttons crossed to the small window and tried to open it by way of response. He muttered under his breath. Aloud he said, "It's still jammed."

Cressida waved one hand at him. "Oh, I was going to get Bradley to fix it. That poor man."

"And that's our cue," I said to Mr Buttons. "Let's get to it."

Cressida placed her laptop on the old secretaire. Made of oak, it was a beautiful piece, Victorian era and imported from England by Cressida's great grandmother. "Allow me to type," Mr Buttons said, sitting on the high-backed throne chair before Cressida or I had a chance to do so.

He opened the laptop and tapped away at the keys. Cressida and I leant over his shoulder. "Have you found anything yet?" Cressida said.

Mr Buttons sighed. "My dear lady, please allow me a few minutes before you ask again. On second thoughts, please do not ask again. I shall inform you the moment I uncover anything of interest."

By the fifth page, Mr Buttons hadn't uncovered anything, and I was beginning to think it was a waste of time. I turned away, and looked at Lord Farringdon who was sauntering into the room. "Eureka!" Mr Buttons exclaimed, startling me.

I looked over his shoulder at the screen, and gasped.

Cressida leant so close to the screen that her nose nearly touched it. "I can't believe it! It *is* him, isn't it?"

"He's many years younger, but it's clearly him," I said.

Mr Buttons jabbed his finger on the screen. "There's his name, written right under the photograph. Detective Dennis Stanton."

"So Dennis was one of the detectives on the robbery case all those years ago," I said slowly, trying to process at all. "Well, that adds up now, with the real estate agents saying that they've never heard of him."

"I'm not sure I follow your reasoning," Mr Buttons said, turning around to face me.

"Dennis is either the murderer or he's here for another reason," I said. "He obviously came to the boarding house to keep an eye on Bradley. He was pretending to look for a house to buy as a cover."

"Of course, he himself could be the murderer," Cressida said.

I agreed. "We can't rule anyone out. I should tell Blake that Dennis was involved in the case."

Mr Buttons touched my arm. "Do you think that's wise, Sibyl? He'll ask how you became privy to the information."

I rubbed my forehead. "Oh dear, you're right, Mr Buttons. What should we do now?"

"I think we should challenge Adrian and tell him we know he's not working for the Office of Geographic Names," Cressida said. "Then we should challenge Wendy Mason and tell her we know she didn't go gold panning that day and ask her who the two men are. Then we could tell Dennis that we know he was on the bank robbery case and was one of those who put Bradley in prison.

Mr Buttons stood up abruptly. "My dear woman, you'll do nothing of the sort. It will be altogether too dangerous. If one of the boarders is the murderer, then saying such things will put your life in danger."

"So you don't think the chef is the murderer anymore?" I asked him.

Before Mr Buttons could answer, Cressida butted in. "Oh yes! I will tell Albert that we know he's not really French."

Mr Buttons threw his hands in the air. "Cressida Upthorpe! Haven't you heard a thing I've said? It's simply not safe to question anyone."

To my surprise, Cressida agreed. "You're right, Mr Buttons, I suppose. Let's look for more information on Dennis. That might throw some light on the case."

Mr Buttons returned to his chair, satisfied, but Cressida winked at me. I wondered what she was up to. I soon found out. "I'm just going to make a nice pot of tea," she said. "Sibyl, would you like to help me make the sandwiches?"

"Sure," I said, casting a sideways glance at Mr Buttons to see if he knew she was up to something. It seemed that he did not. He was bending over the computer, staring at the screen.

As soon as Cressida and I were out of the room, she whispered to me, "This investigation has stalled, and those detectives are useless. You and I are going to have to take matters into our own hands, Sibyl."

"I'm not sure I like the sound of that, Cressida," I said. "Our track record of confronting murderers hasn't done us much good in the past."

"Pish posh!" Cressida took my arm and steered me towards the dining room. "Who should we start with, Adrian or Wendy?"

The matter was decided for us, as Adrian was sitting at the dining table, reading his iPad and sipping from a cup. He looked up when we entered the room, his brow furrowed. "You said you want to start with me?"

Cressida and I exchanged glances. "Yes, there's something we've found out," Cressida said. She crossed to the dining table and beckoned for me to sit next to her. "Adrian, do you mind if I come straight to the point?"

He seemed a bit nervous, but shook his head.

"We found out that you're not working for the Office of Geographic Names. There's no such office in New South Wales. Here it's called the Geographical Names Board. It's only called the Office of Geographic Names in Victoria."

Adrian laughed nervously. "Silly me. I used to work for the Office of Geographic Names in Victoria when I first moved to Australia, so I got used to calling it that."

"The game's up, I'm afraid, Adrian," Cressida said, sounding for all the world like a mob boss. "We've spoken to the council, who confirmed that there is no one in town from any such organisation. We'd like to know why you've told us such a big lie, and what you're really here for. Perhaps we need to call the police and tell them. Did you murder Bradley Brown?"

I managed to recover to the point that I shut my gaping jaw. I was shocked that she was so forthright. It seemed I was not the only one who was shocked. "No, I didn't!" Adrian exclaimed. He wrung his hands and slouched in his seat.

"Well then, why did you invent such a story?" Cressida pressed him. "Who do you really work for?"

"I'm a journalist," he said shakily.

"Aha!" I elbowed Cressida. "Mr Buttons guessed he was a journalist." To Adrian, I said, "Were you doing a story on Bradley?"

Adrian shook his head. "I didn't know a thing about Bradley, not until after he died. No, I'm writing a book on the Nithwell family of England."

"Then why did you feel the need to keep that a secret?" Cressida asked.

Adrian leant back in his seat. "Because of Mr Buttons, obviously."

Cressida and I exchanged glances once more. "What on earth does Mr Buttons have to do with it?" I asked him.

"You don't know?" He quirked one eyebrow. When Cressida and I remained silent, he pressed on. "Mr Buttons is Lord Nithwell, the Fifteenth Earl of Nithwell."

At that point, the dining room door flung open, and Mr Buttons stood there, illuminated by the filtered sunlight behind him.

He did not speak, and I held my breath, wondering how he would react. I wondered if he would be angry. So this was his secret! He must have known all along that Adrian knew, and that was why he was so uncomfortable with him, especially when Adrian was taunting him.

To my relief, Mr Buttons meekly crossed the room and sat at the table. "So my secret is finally out," he lamented, "after all these years of me being so careful to keep my identity hidden. I abandoned my life of privilege and simply wanted to live as a commoner in Australia. Was that too much to ask?" He rested his head in his hands.

"Do you have family looking for you?" I asked him.

He shook his head. "Not family, but custodians." He glared at Adrian.

Adrian held up both hands, palms facing outwards. "I'm only doing my job. I've got to make a living. Lord Nithwell, I can't write that book without you. Plus you're the most interesting person in it. It will be quite a boring book without you."

I noticed that Mr Buttons looked somewhat pleased by that remark. Adrian was still talking. "Your family's history is fascinating, but many people don't consider *any* history to be interesting. Now, the chapter on you will be fascinating. How many Earls have left their homeland and gone to live in Australia, especially in a small country town where nothing ever happens?"

"Except murders," I couldn't resist adding.

Adrian ignored me. "Lord Nithwell, please let me interview you. I won't mention that you're living in Little Tatterford; I'll just say that you're living in outback Australia."

"Little Tatterford is hardly the outback," Cressida said, visibly annoyed.

Adrian shrugged one shoulder. "It sounds better that way," he said dismissively. "Lord Nithwell, if you will allow me to interview you, I'll keep you as anonymous as I can in the book."

I wondered if there was a threat implicit in that statement. It seemed to me that Adrian was implying that if Mr Buttons did not allow him to interview him, then he would write up

Mr Buttons' story in the book and tell everyone he was in Little Tatterford.

It seemed the same thought had occurred to Mr Buttons. "I agree to your terms, but I'll have my lawyer draw up a contract to that effect. Also, you are never to call me Lord Nithwell again. You are to call me Mr Buttons."

Adrian smirked. "You've got a deal." He held out his hand. Mr Buttons pulled a white linen handkerchief from his pocket, wiped Adrian's hand, and then shook it.

"So you're not the murderer then?" Cressida said, disappointment evident in her voice.

Chef Dubois walked into the room, carrying a silver teapot. "Murderer?" he echoed.

"We have just ascertained that Adrian Addison here is not a murderer, but a journalist," Mr Buttons said in a steely tone. "Chef Dubois, would you kindly take a seat?"

The man looked terrified. He put the teapot down on the table. "You want me to sit?" he asked nervously.

"Yes," Mr Buttons said.

The chef took a seat. He looked far more nervous than Adrian when Cressida had confronted him only minutes earlier.

"We all know that you're not French," Mr Buttons said. "Did you murder Bradley Brown?"

The chef clutched his throat. "No! No, of course not!"

Mr Buttons leant across the table. "You can drop the fake French accent, my good man. You're no more French than I am. I am sure you have never even been to Paris. Come clean, or it will be the worse for you."

"You're scaring him, Mr Buttons," Cressida said. "Please don't be upset, Chef Dubois. You don't have to be French to keep your job here. I want you to stay on as chef."

"Good gracious me. You can't have a murderer as a chef, Cressida!" Mr Buttons' voice rose to a high pitch.

"I didn't murder anyone," Chef Dubois said, although he had dropped the French accent. "I'm so sorry I lied, Cressida. My qualifications aren't the best, and I don't have any good references, so I thought if I pretended I was French, you wouldn't bother to check international references."

Mr Buttons made a strangling sound. "Cressida was hardly likely to check international references in person. There are such things as email and international calls," he added sarcastically.

"Mr Buttons is just a little upset at the moment," Cressida said in a placating tone. "Pay him no mind. Of course you'll keep your job, but not if you murdered Bradley Brown."

"I didn't murder anyone," Chef Dubois said again. "I truly apologise for lying about my qualifications, but I didn't murder anyone."

I had forgotten that Adrian was there. He looked fascinated by the whole exchange. I certainly hoped he didn't put that in his book. It struck me that we only had his word that he was a journalist. Perhaps he was the murderer, after all. Still, it would be strange for him to say he was working for the Office of Geographic Names as a cover story for the fact that he was a journalist writing a book on Mr Buttons' family, which in turn was a cover story for the fact that he was a murderer. I shook my head and smiled to myself. No, that would be too far-fetched.

And then again, was Chef Dubois the murderer? Perhaps he had a connection to Bradley that we didn't know about. It was time we spoke to Wendy Mason.

16

"I'm glad Chef Dubois isn't the murderer," Cressida said, after the three of us were back in the private living room.

Mr Buttons looked most put out. "I still reserve judgement on that one."

Cressida shook her head and bent down to stroke Lord Farringdon. Cat hair flew in all directions. "No, Lord Farringdon has always maintained that Chef Dubois is innocent. He vouches for him."

Mr Buttons' eyes narrowed, but he said nothing. I think he was transfixed by the cat hair.

"So, Mr Buttons, I'm surprised to know that you're an Earl." I considered how to word it before I asked him, and I thought that preferable to demanding to know why he hadn't told us.

Mr Buttons lowered himself gently into one of the antique chairs, this one upholstered in an unpleasant shade of mustard damask jacquard fabric. Lord Farringdon had been about to leap into that very seat, so he shot Mr Buttons a filthy glare. Mr Buttons wrung his hands nervously and looked at the floor. "I came to Australia to escape my past," he said in a small voice.

Cressida stood over him and folded her arms. "Mr Buttons, here I was thinking we didn't have any secrets from each other. I must say, I'm most disappointed in you. And escaping your past? It makes you sound like you're a criminal."

"I like my life here," Mr Buttons protested. "And people always treat me differently once they find out that I'm an Earl. Here I can be carefree, with no responsibilities, and no need to keep up the act. I'm a simple person, really."

"You still could have told me." Cressida sounded quite hurt.

"I apologise. It's just that I thought you would act differently around me."

Cressida flung her arms skywards. "Why would I? I don't even know what an Earl is!"

"An Earl is a member of the nobility," Mr Buttons said automatically. "It's above a Viscount and below a Marquess."

Cressida was not placated. "I don't even know what a Marquess is!"

"A Marquess is above an Earl and below a Duke," Mr Buttons said, and then he muttered something about Visigoths and Lombards. At least, I think that's what he said. It gave me flashbacks of my school days.

Cressida was about to say something else, and by the look on her face, I could see it wasn't going to be good. To divert her attention, I said, "Why don't we go and speak with Wendy Mason? We could say we just happened to see her in Pharmidale that day when she said she was panning for gold."

As soon as I said it, I realised that Mr Buttons had recently objected to such a plan, and I was surprised when he did not object now. Clearly, he was too upset about being outed as a member of the nobility. He stood up, said, "Okay," in a small voice, and then made for the door. Cressida stormed after him.

I hurried past them and blocked the exit. "Now then, we'll have to put our hurts and differences aside, because we need to be calm to speak to Wendy. Don't forget, she could well be the murderer. Do you both agree?" I was actually addressing my remarks to Cressida.

They both nodded, although Cressida still looked upset. "Where would Wendy be now?" I asked them.

"Not panning for gold," Mr Buttons said snarkily.

"I think I saw her car outside when we came back," Cressida said. "We can't all go to her room, because that would be too confrontational, yet we need to speak to her alone."

"Why don't you just pop up to her room and ask her to join us for a drink in the private living room?" I suggested.

"That's a good idea." Cressida gathered her bright red skirts and took off at a fast pace.

"She's still angry with me," Mr Buttons lamented. "Are you angry with me, Sibyl?"

I hurried to reassure him. "Of course not, Mr Buttons. Cressida is just upset because she thought the two of you were best friends. She's a little shaken to think that you were keeping something so big from her. She'll get over it soon."

"I'm not so sure I share your confidence." Mr Buttons' face fell even further.

I patted him lightly on his back. "Cressida isn't one to hold a grudge. You'll see! Now let's go and sit down and try to look casual. Do you have any idea how we can work into the subject?"

Before Mr Buttons could answer, Cressida hurried back into the room. "She's right behind me," she said in a stage whisper. The three of us all but sprinted to our seats.

Moments later, Wendy poked her head around the door. "Oh, I see this is the right room."

"Yes, it is." Mr Buttons held up a brandy balloon. "What would you like to drink? And please sit down." He gestured to an uncomfortable looking mahogany balloon back chair. Wendy sat upright on the chair. Our intent to make this look casual wasn't off to a good start. She already looked like she was being interrogated, if not tortured, perched on the high chair while all of us were leaning back in comfortable, albeit unattractive, armchairs.

"This is quite unusual decor," Wendy said, looking around the room in alarm.

"Thank you." Cressida beamed at her, obviously thinking her words were a compliment. "So, Wendy, have you found any more gold?"

Mr Buttons spoke before Wendy had a chance to do so. "Wendy, we know you weren't panning for gold. You see, I just happened to be in a café in Pharmidale and saw you speaking to two men on the very day you told us you were gold panning. What's more, they were two men who were at the funeral, yet you did not interact with them at all on that day."

Cressida nodded. "And I saw you coming out of a tourist shop in Pharmidale not long before Mr Buttons saw you. The lady in there told us you had bought that gold you pretended you found in the creek."

Wendy leant forward and put her head in her hands. "Oh no. I was hoping no one would find out. I didn't think it would be so easy to blow my cover." When she straightened up, her face was bright red. "Okay then, you got me. I confess."

"You murdered Bradley Brown?" Cressida said in shock.

Wendy looked even more startled. Her hand flew to her throat. "Oh goodness gracious me, no! Certainly not! I didn't murder anyone!"

"Then why the pretence?" I asked her.

She sighed long and hard. "If I tell you, I must have your word that it doesn't leave this room."

We all nodded. She pushed on. "I'm an insurance investigator."

"An insurance investigator?" Cressida said, frowning.

"Yes, I'm working for the bank's insurance company—you know, the bank that Bradley Brown robbed?"

"We know all about it." Mr Buttons waved her on.

"Then you know he got away with millions and it hasn't been found to this day. I came to Little Tatterford to see if I could uncover the money. I heard he did a lot of work for this establishment, so I booked myself in here under the guise of a woman being on a holiday, panning for gold."

"Does Adrian know you're an investigator?" I asked her.

She looked startled, and then recovered quickly. "No, not at all."

"Had you met Adrian before you came to the boarding house?" Mr Buttons asked her.

She shook her head. "No, I had never met him before. I met him for the first time the morning of the murder." She looked at each one of us in turn. "Is that what this is all about? You really think I murdered Bradley Brown?"

Mr Buttons sputtered, and Cressida fumbled with her hands, so I answered. "Yes, you were one of our suspects, to tell you the truth," I said.

Instead of being offended, she smiled. "And you're concerned because the murder happened on your property, and those detectives are worse than useless?"

"That's exactly right!" Cressida said with feeling. "If you didn't do it, do you have any idea who did?"

"I thought it might be either Adrian or the chef," she said. "And please keep this to yourselves too, but Dennis Stanton is a retired detective."

We all nodded. "We know," I said. "He was on the team that had Bradley sentenced for the robbery."

Wendy clutched her stomach. "Well, this has just been one shock after another. I didn't know you knew so much. Yes, Dennis has given me some helpful information."

"Have the two of you been working together?" I asked her.

She shook her head again. "No, but when I arrived at the boarding house, I recognised him. I've lived and breathed nothing else since my firm assigned me to the case. Dennis offered to help out. It was obvious to me that he was here for the same reason."

"He's working for your insurance company, too?" Cressida asked her.

She shook her head. "No. From what he said, I gathered it was unfinished business. He feels bad that the money was never found. He doesn't feel comfortable retiring without all the loose ends tied up."

I thought it over. If it wasn't Wendy, and it wasn't Dennis, then it did only leave the chef or Adrian. I still wasn't ruling out the possibility that two or more people were in it together.

"It isn't Chef Dubois," Cressida said firmly. "Lord Farringdon vouched for him. I keep saying that, but nobody will listen to me."

"Who is Lord Farringdon?" Wendy asked.

Mr Buttons at once stood up. "Thank you for your help, madam. We will certainly keep what you told us in the strictest confidence." He offered her his arm, and then hurried her to the door. He opened the door for her, and then watched her walk away.

Mr Buttons hurried back to us. "I know who the murderer is!" he announced.

17

I held my breath. "Who is it?" I asked him.

"It's obvious, isn't it? Chef Dubois. I've been saying that all the time."

Cressida and I groaned. "It's Dorothy all over again," Cressida muttered.

"What makes you think it's the chef?" I asked him.

Mr Buttons puffed out his chest. "Didn't you hear Wendy? If we can believe that she is not the murderer, and that Dennis has been assisting her, then it stands to reason that it's either the chef or Adrian Addison." He pointed to Cressida and then to me. "The two of you both told me that Bradley was alarmed when he recognised someone in the dining room. Have you forgotten?"

"Yes, but we can't remember whether the chef was in the room at the time," I said. "Please don't take offence, Mr Buttons, but I think accusing the chef is something of a wild leap."

Mr Buttons looked most disgruntled.

"And just because Wendy says she isn't the murderer, doesn't mean she isn't," I continued. "I really don't think we're any further along. Maybe we're going about this the wrong way."

Cressida and Mr Buttons looked at me expectantly. I took a few moments to compose my thoughts, and then said, "Perhaps we should look at people who had a reason to kill him. I think we should approach it from that angle." I walked over to sit in one of the comfortable chairs, and Cressida and Mr Buttons did likewise. Lord Farringdon had taken the chair Mr Buttons had been sitting in previously, so Mr Buttons sat in the one next to it.

I scratched my head. "Okay then, let's throw up some hypotheticals. Who would have a reason to kill Bradley? The first thought that occurs to me is the other bank robbers. The police shot them all dead. Surely they have families? What if a family member of one of the other robbers is angry that Bradley escaped unscathed?"

"Or perhaps they're angry that Bradley didn't share the money with them," Mr Buttons said.

Cressida clapped her hands. "We don't know that Bradley didn't share the money with the other families. For all we know, he might have done just that."

I had to agree. "That's a good point, Cressida. Now what are some other reasons that someone would want to kill him?"

"There's always the possibility that it didn't have anything to do with the bank robbery," Mr Buttons said thoughtfully, "but that seems unlikely. No, maybe we should just assume that it *did* have something to do with the robbery."

"And then there's the money," I said. "Perhaps someone murdered him for the millions. It seems the most likely reason to me."

Mr Buttons nodded. "If someone discovered where the money was, then they would have taken the money, and murdered Bradley to tie up loose ends."

Cressida shook her head. "The police looked for that money the entire time Bradley was in jail, and didn't find it. How could someone find it now? It seems unlikely."

I was relieved that Cressida was speaking to Mr Buttons in her normal tone, her previous resentment seemingly forgotten. "Well, I'm all out of ideas," I said sadly. "Can anyone think of anything else?"

No one responded. A heavy silence descended over the room, broken only by the swishing of Lord Farringdon's tail. Mr Buttons finally stood up and crossed back to the throne chair in front of the secretaire. "Let's look through these old records once more. I know it's tenuous, but it's all we have to go on."

For the next fifteen minutes, Cressida and I leant over Mr Buttons' shoulder while he scrolled through all the newspaper reports of the robbery, and then Bradley's sentencing. My eyes felt dry and tight, and when I rubbed them, an eyelash curled over and dug into my eye. "I've got something in my eye," I said urgently. "I'll just go to the bathroom. I'll be right back."

I raced out the door and nearly barrelled right into the non-French chef. I quickly closed the door behind me. "Were you listening in on our conversation?" I said in an accusatory tone. I expected him to deny it, and I was surprised when he didn't.

"Yes," he said. "I wanted to know if Cressida was going to give me my notice. I thought she might be discussing it in there with you and Mr Buttons."

"I'm sure Cressida has absolutely no intention of giving you your notice, but she might if she knows you've been snooping around doors."

He scurried away. If only I could remember whether he had been in the room when Bradley looked shocked. For some reason, that made me think of mangoes. I hurried after him. "Chef Dubois, please don't worry. Cressida won't sack you. Your job is safe."

He looked so relieved that I felt mean for admonishing him for eavesdropping. "There's something that's been bugging me, and I don't know why," I told him. "It's about the mangoes."

He raised one eyebrow. "The mangoes?"

I nodded. "Remember that on the day that Bradley Brown was murdered, you had a box of mangoes on the front porch?"

"Yes, mangoes aren't in season yet," he said. "I did take a risk on one box. I bought some frozen ones from a fruit truck that does the Brisbane to Melbourne run. They looked fine on the outside, but when I opened one, it was horribly unripe. I'm from Queensland, you see, so I'm not used to this climate. Still, mangoes won't even be available in Queensland for weeks yet, so I shouldn't have taken the risk on the box. I put them on the porch to thaw. Unfortunately, the forensics team took them all. It will be weeks before I get mangoes again." He narrowed his eyes. "Why did you want to know?"

I shook my head. "I can't quite remember, to be honest. It's just something that's been bugging me. You know how something is just on the tip of your mind and you can't remember what it is?"

He nodded. "I don't like it when that happens."

"So did you eat any of the mangoes?"

He chuckled. "There's no way anyone could have eaten one of those unripe mangoes. They were white-green inside. They wouldn't have been ripe for ages."

I remembered seeing the body, not a pleasant memory, but I did recall that the mango stuffed in his mouth was a strange pale green, not the usual vibrant golden colour. I thanked the chef and left. When I reached the bathroom, I realised the eyelash had worked its way out of my eye, and my eye was no longer stinging. Nevertheless, I dabbed some water on it for good measure and then returned to the room.

Cressida ran over and grasped me by both shoulders. "Sibyl! Mr Buttons and I think we've made a wonderful discovery! We've broken open the case."

I gasped. "You know who the murderer is?"

Cressida's face fell. "Well... no. Still, we've made a wonderful breakthrough."

"Tremendous, tremendous," Mr Buttons muttered to himself. He looked over his shoulder at me. "Come, Sibyl, you must see this!"

I hurried over and looked at the screen. "Isn't that the photo we saw earlier?" I asked, puzzled.

"Yes, but that's not all!" Cressida pointed to the screen. "Show her, Mr Buttons." Before he could do so, she yelled, "Stop! I haven't shown Sibyl the woman."

"What woman?" I asked her.

Cressida tapped her finger on the screen, but Mr Buttons objected. "Cressida, my dear woman, I must inform you that not only is this a touchscreen, but I have just cleaned the screen, and so touching it is not advisable."

"Sorry," Cressida said meekly. She pointed to the photo on the screen, making sure not to touch the screen this time. "Who is she?" I asked Cressida.

"We don't know, but she's in a lot of photos," Mr Buttons said. "Have a look at this."

It was then I noticed he had about fifty or so tabs opened on the laptop. As he went through each one in turn, I saw that they were all photographs, and indeed, the woman was in the background of each one of them. I expressed that aloud, but Mr Buttons said, "We did find several photographs that did not feature her, but we thought there was no point showing them to you."

I nodded. "That makes sense. You don't have any idea who she is?"

"We don't know her name or where she lives, but she was clearly someone important to Bradley. She's in the background of photos of all his court appearances, both inside the courtroom and on the street when the police are taking him away."

I narrowed my eyes. "Didn't we find out that Bradley didn't have any family?"

"That's right." Mr Buttons pointed towards the screen. "And if he *did* have any family, then the police would have soon found out. I suspect this woman was his girlfriend, because if she was his wife, then of course the police would know about it. Maybe this woman is the one with all the cash from the robbery."

"Now all we have to do is find her," I said dryly.

"She lives in Little Tatterford," Cressida said.

Mr Buttons jumped and I gasped. "You know her?" I asked her.

Cressida shook her head. "No."

"My goodness gracious me," Mr Buttons said. "Out with it, woman! Please refrain from keeping us in suspense in this unseemly manner."

"In one of the photos, she was holding a brown paper bag that had the words *Five Goats Soap* stamped on it."

"What photo was that?" Mr Buttons asked in a disbelieving tone.

"Hop off the chair and I'll show you." Mr Buttons did as he was asked, and in no time at all Cressida had found the photo. She dabbed her finger on the screen and then turned to Mr Buttons. "Sorry. But there it is. Look."

I peered at the screen. Sure enough, Cressida was right. "What does that mean?" I asked her.

"*Five Goats Soap* is a local Little Tatterford business," Cressida said. "It's been going since the mid 1980s. I occasionally run into the owner when I'm having my eyebrows waxed. She goes to my beauty therapist."

"Well done, Cressida," Mr Buttons said, beaming from ear to ear.

"I hate to be the one to throw a dampener on this happy party," I said, "but it doesn't mean that this woman still lives in Little Tatterford."

"Oh, yes she does," Cressida said in a matter-of-fact voice. "I often see her at the local supermarket."

I was struck speechless, but Mr Buttons apparently was made of stronger stuff. "Well, why didn't you tell us so, woman?" he bellowed. "All this conversation as to whether she was in Little Tatterford or not, and you knew all along that she was."

Cressida smiled, as if Mr Buttons had been complimenting her. "Yes, I did," she said cheerily. "I recognised her. I know she's one of those people who live out on the Surrender Road, on one of those big, unproductive farms. They're all ferals out there," she added with a shake of her head. "They'll shoot you as soon as look at you."

"And I suppose you're going to suggest that we go and visit her," Mr Buttons said in a voice dripping with sarcasm.

Cressida's smile grew wider. "Yes, that's right."

18

I had no desire to visit a gun-toting woman who was possibly the accomplice of a notorious criminal, and worse still, might be sitting on his ill-gotten millions. At first I thought I was quite safe, given that Cressida only knew the general location of the woman's farm. I thought she'd never find out the woman's address, and even if she did, it would probably take weeks. Sadly, I wasn't reckoning on the Little Tatterford rumour mill.

Mr Buttons and I were sitting in Cressida's car, while Cressida was showing the photo she had made Mr Buttons print to one of the local hairdressers. "Do you think the hairdresser will know where this woman lives?" I asked Mr Buttons.

"I certainly hope not!" he said fervently. "I really don't want to visit this woman. She sounds dangerous, by all accounts."

"I'm with you, Mr Buttons."

Cressida returned to the car, waving the print-out at us. She jumped in behind the steering wheel. "Cheryl knows her address!"

Mr Buttons and I both groaned. "Please tell me that hairdresser doesn't do the woman's hair?" Mr Buttons said. "And if so, please tell me her hair doesn't look like it did in that old photograph. Her hair style was most indecorous."

Cressida laughed. "Of course not. The mysterious woman is called Bertha Ward. Cheryl said that Bertha doesn't go to any of the hairdressers in town."

"I'm probably going to regret asking this," I said, "but how does Cheryl know anything about Bertha, if Bertha isn't a client?"

"Cheryl's husband, Tom, has pig dogs, and he goes out shooting with Bertha most weekends, of course."

"Of course," Mr Buttons muttered. "Where are you going?" he asked in alarm as Cressida started the car.

"To Bertha's."

Mr Buttons leant over to look at me in the back seat. His face had gone white. "Say something, Sibyl," he said in alarm.

"Cressida, I don't think we should go out there, given that we're unarmed and everything." I heard my voice come out as a squeak.

Cressida laughed at me. "She won't hurt us. She might be rude and unfriendly, that's all." She pulled the car out into the traffic and headed south on the highway.

"Do you know how to get out to Surrender Road?" I asked, hoping she would get lost on the way.

"Everyone knows how to get to Surrender Road," Cressida said. "Ferals live out there."

"So you said." I looked in my handbag for my phone. Maybe I should tell Blake where I was going, so he could send reinforcements. "Cressida, you do realise this woman could very well be hiding millions of dollars, and so she won't take kindly to us going out there. She could easily shoot us all," I added for clarity.

"Oh, do you really think so?" Cressida said calmly, as she turned right onto Queens Road. "This road runs into Surrender Road after about twenty five kilometres."

"I don't suppose there's any chance you would turn around and go back if we both pleaded with you?" Mr Buttons said.

Cressida laughed as if he had made the most hilarious joke, and accelerated. It seemed like an age before we reached Surrender Road. The scenery along Queens Road was rather boring, big granite boulders and bush giving way to long, low paddocks full of sheep. We hit dirt as soon as Queens Road became Surrender Road. The red dirt seeped in through the car, causing no end of distress for Mr Buttons.

After half an hour or so, Cressida slowed the car. "Now keep a lookout, both of you. The property name is *Wallaby Run*."

"I can't see anything through all this dust," Mr Buttons spluttered.

Moments later, my head just missed slamming into the back of Mr Buttons' seat as Cressida suddenly applied the brakes. "We almost passed it," she said. "Wasn't it lucky I spotted it!"

Mr Buttons and I remained silent. Cressida swung the car hard right and pulled up in front of a derelict gate. A sign, with the words *Wallaby Run* roughly scrawled in what looked like a marker pen, was propped up against the wooden post which had seen better days.

"I'll get the gate," I said. It took every last bit of my strength to drag the gate open. I wondered if Bertha Ward was injecting herself with cattle steroids. When Cressida drove through, I managed to drag the gate shut and then hook the wire loop over a steel post to secure it. My biceps and triceps were burning from the effort. I coughed as the dust kicked up by the car eddied around my face and into my mouth.

When I got back in the car, I said, "I suppose we should have thought how we should approach this on the way here."

"I had lots of thoughts," Mr Buttons said, "but none of them were good."

"Leave all the talking to me," Cressida said. She took off, a little too fast for the road which was filled with potholes, some so big I wondered if we could lose a tyre.

"How far to the house?" Mr Buttons said after we had been going for five minutes.

Cressida did not need to answer, because we rounded a bend, and there was the house. Cressida slowed the car, and parked in front of the house. "I don't think we should knock on the back door," she said. "We don't want to frighten her."

"Maybe we should all stay in the car and wait until she comes out to us," I said.

Soon, any thoughts of getting out of the car were put to rest by the pack of dogs that suddenly appeared, all barking ferociously and showing their fangs. I instinctively locked my car door.

The dust cleared, and in front of me I saw a large rifle. It was being held by a hefty, burly woman. She was wearing a floral print dress and knee length gumboots, and a wide straw hat. It's a wonder I even noticed that, because the rifle was pointed straight at us. The dogs stopped barking and all ran to stand behind her.

Cressida got out of the car, despite our protests. "Hi, I'm Cressida Upthorpe from the boarding house in town," she said in a loud voice. "Bradley Brown was murdered on my porch."

I shook my head. Of all the things to say to a gun-toting woman on steroids!

The woman remained silent, which I took as a good sign. She had not shot at us yet. Cressida must have taken the lack of gunfire as encouragement, because she added, "I'm here with Mr Buttons, who is my permanent boarder, and Sibyl, who rents a cottage from me. They're good friends of mine, and we're concerned that our lives might be in danger. The three of us are investigating Bradley's murder, because the detectives are worse than useless."

The woman lowered her gun marginally, and slowly walked over to us. She was walking in the same way that she would stalk a wild animal. She jerked the gun. "Get out of the car, you two."

I took a deep breath and got out of the car. Mr Buttons did likewise. Bertha edged around. "The three of you stand over there," she said motioning with the gun. She glanced inside the car quickly. "What did you say your name was again?"

"Cressida Upthorpe. Bradley was doing odd jobs for me."

Bertha walked over to Cressida. "Yes, he told me. Can you vouch for these two?"

"Absolutely," Cressida said. "They are dear friends of mine."

Bertha lowered the rifle to her side. "Were you followed?"

"No," Cressida said. "We haven't seen a car in miles."

Bertha nodded. "Well then, you'd better come inside for a cuppa."

My knees went weak with relief.

Mr Buttons and I clutched each other and fell in behind Bertha and Cressida, who were striding towards the house. The house looked like any other in these parts—low, wooden, and tired, with a wraparound porch, and painted in an unattractive and unremarkable shade of pale blue.

Gumboots were strewn all over the porch, and various Siamese cats were curled up, asleep. Bertha must have seen me looking at the cats, because she said, "They're my pet cats. The farm cats don't come up to the house." She pointed out towards the closest barn, where several cats were curled up in the sun, asleep. One of the big black and white dogs had followed us onto the porch. A Siamese cat stood up, arched her back, and hissed at him. The dog put his tail between his legs and ran away, scattering the chooks in all directions. "My Siamese cats are vicious," Bertha said proudly. "Come in. No need to take off your shoes."

I was expecting the interior of the house to match the exterior, but I was mistaken. The door opened onto the foyer, the floor of which was covered by even more gumboots, and from the pegs on the walls hung various oilskins and coats as well as a stockwhip. The foyer in turn opened onto the kitchen, and that was a surprise. Every manner of stainless steel European appliance graced the room. There were two dishwashers, a huge double door fridge, a very expensive coffee machine, and various other appliances. I found it rather incongruous, because the old bench tops were made of laminate, and a Formica and metal table from the 1950s sat in the middle of the room. At any rate, I could easily see where some of the bank robbery funds had gone.

Bertha poured water into the jug. "I'll put the billy on," she said. While the jug was boiling, she opened a plastic container and tipped a large pile of biscuits onto a plate. "Anzac biscuits—I made them myself."

She was still eyeing us warily, but her manner was friendly enough and she was no longer threatening to shoot us. I could feel the tension slowly leaving my body. She poured us all a cup of black tea and then sat at the kitchen table with us. "Now why have you come to see me?"

Mr Buttons and I shot Cressida a warning look, but either she didn't see us, or she didn't care. "We think Bradley hid the robbery money at your place."

I gasped, and judged the distance from Bertha to her rifle, which was propped up next to her refrigerator. "We don't care what you do with the money," I hastened to add. "It's just that we think you might be in danger if you've got it. We're also worried that we're in danger, because whoever murdered Bradley must be looking for the money."

To my enormous relief, Bertha kept her seat. She pointed to Cressida. "Bradley told me if anything happened to him, I could count on you. He said you gave him a chance when no one else would. You were always good to him."

She pulled a tissue from her pocket and dabbed at her eyes.

Once more, Cressida came straight to the point. "Do you know who murdered him?"

Bertha bit her lip. "The police don't know I exist," she said. "Bradley and I were never legally married. He always knew he was going to get caught, but he said he'd make hay while the sun shone. He went to great lengths to keep me out of the public eye. If anyone thinks I've got the money, they will certainly come for me. I'm ready for them, though." She pointed to an army issue metal chest on the floor. "That's full of grenades, and various other useful items. Bradley had connections."

I fought the urge to sprint from the house. "I have security cameras all around too," she added, "but you'd never spot them. It was hard for me, Bradley being in prison all those years, and as soon as he got out, some scumbag topped him."

"Do you know who murdered Bradley?" Cressida asked once more.

Bertha sipped from her cup before speaking. "Bradley always said the less I know, the better off I'd be. He told me that someone came to see him and demanded half the money."

"Did he say whether it was a man or a woman?" I asked her.

She looked surprised at the question. "It was a man," she said, "but Bradley didn't tell me his name. What this man didn't know was that Bradley had given a share to the families of the other five men in his gang. Bradley didn't have all the money left." She laughed. "He had a lot, mind you, but he didn't have it all. This man threatened to turn him in to the police for the reward if he didn't give him substantially more than the reward amount."

"And did he?" Mr Buttons appeared to be no longer afraid, and was hanging on her every word.

She nodded sadly. "I think that's why he was murdered. He was at a loose end, you see."

"Just before Bradley was murdered, he came into the dining room. He looked shocked to see the three new boarders," Cressida told her.

"And we don't know if Cressida's chef was in the room at the time," I told her.

Cressida nodded. "The boarders are Adrian Addison, Wendy Mason, and Dennis Stanton."

Bertha sat bolt upright. "Dennis Stanton was one of the police who gave evidence against Bradley at his trial."

We all nodded. "And Wendy Mason is an insurance investigator working for the bank that was robbed," I added. "But considering

Bradley said a man was blackmailing him, then it had to be either the retired cop, Dennis Stanton, or Adrian Addison, who is writing a book."

"Or the chef," Mr Buttons added. "Albert Dubois, or whatever his real name is."

"Well, at least we've narrowed the suspects down," I said, trying to remain positive.

"You can't come back out here," Bertha said, "but I'll give you my phone number, and you give me yours." She addressed that remark to Cressida. "If anyone finds out where the money is, it'll be curtains for me just like it was for Bradley." Her voice broke.

On the drive back to the gate, I said, "I feel really sorry for Bertha. She's obviously done it tough."

"Notice she didn't actually admit to having the money," Mr Buttons said.

"She obviously does," I said. "She pretty much said she did."

"We don't know that, and I don't think we should mention that to the police," Cressida said. "That poor woman. She's out in the middle of nowhere, running this big place by herself. It must be a lonely life. She would have been so excited when Bradley got out of prison after all those years, and then he was murdered. "

"I hope she's safe," I said, "and I hope the detectives somehow manage to solve the case before anyone comes looking for her."

Cressida stopped at the gate. "We've made progress. At least we now know the murderer was a man."

Mr Buttons muttered to himself.

19

By the time we got back to the boarding house, we were no closer to discovering the murderer. I wanted to go back to my cottage, but Cressida didn't like the sound of that idea.

"We're close, I just know we are," she said, rubbing her temples furiously.

Mr Buttons held one finger to his mouth. "The walls have ears. Let us convene to the private living room."

"Is there any point going over it one more time?" I asked them. "We have just talked about it at some length, and we haven't come up with anything."

"I agree with Cressida," Mr Buttons said. "We need to put our heads together."

"But we've already done that," I said, stating the obvious. Still, I could see I was defeated, so I followed them into the garishly decorated living room. "Oh that reminds me, I finished a new painting the other day," Cressida said. "Would you like to see it?"

Mr Buttons and I said, "No!" in unison.

Cressida merely shrugged one shoulder. "Should we fetch a pot of tea and some sandwiches before our discussion?"

"How about we give it half an hour, and if we don't come up with anything, we'll officially give up for the day and have some sandwiches then," I said.

To my relief, the other two agreed to my time limit. Mr Buttons and Cressida launched into an animated discussion as to whether or not the French chef was the perpetrator, while I leant back in my chair and closed my eyes. When there was a pause in the conversation, I spoke up. "We know it wasn't Wendy because Bertha said it was a man, and I very much doubt that it's Adrian. He *is* genuinely writing a book on Mr Buttons' family. That only leaves Albert Dubois and Dennis Stanton."

"Then that only leaves Dennis Stanton," Cressida said, "given that Lord Farringdon vouchers for Chef Dubois."

I expected Mr Buttons to disagree vehemently, but to my surprise, he tapped his chin, and then said, "Dennis *did* know all about the money from the bank robbery. He could have been waiting for Bradley to get out of prison for years, just so he could blackmail him."

Cressida agreed. "You know, I think we've been looking at this too closely and going over and over until we've gone into a head spin. Wendy and Dennis were the two who knew all about the bank robbery and how much money was involved. There's still a chance that Wendy was working with someone else, but the fact remains that it was a man who demanded the money from Bradley. The one person who makes sense at this point is Dennis."

"Mangoes!" I jumped to my feet, excited. "That was it!"

Mr Buttons and Cressida looked startled. "Explain yourself, dear girl," Mr Buttons said, waving a hand at me to continue.

I bit my little fingernail. "Well, it's not proof as such, but there is something that struck me as strange, though I couldn't remember what it was." I wanted to pause to get my thoughts together, but I knew Mr Buttons did not like to be kept in suspense. "Remember that Bradley was murdered by an unripe mango?"

Mr Buttons shook his head. "To the contrary, Sibyl, he was strangled with a piece of thin wire."

I shook my head. "No, no, no. You know what I mean. He had a mango shoved in his mouth. Whether or not he was murdered with it is not the point."

"Why didn't you say so?" Mr Buttons looked perplexed.

"Mr Buttons, please give Sibyl a chance to speak."

Mr Buttons made a zipping sign across his mouth.

"Do you remember that it was an unripe mango?"

Cressida and Mr Buttons nodded. "Yes, it was most unripe," Mr Buttons said. "It was an altogether unpleasant shade, somewhere between white and pale green. I almost thought it was one of those strange tropical fruits that are found in Australia, but I knew from its skin that it was a mango."

"Now, did any of the boarders see the mangoes?"

Cressida and Mr Buttons exchanged glances. "No, I don't think so. Did the forensics team confiscate the whole box?" Mr Buttons said.

Cressida nodded vigorously. "That's right. They took the whole box, and then they took the bits of mango from his mouth and from the porch around him."

"So are you all absolutely sure that the boarders didn't see the mango?"

"Indubitably," Mr Buttons said.

Cressida agreed. "Without a doubt."

I waved my finger at them. "When I was walking with Dennis around the garden the other day, we were talking about plants and how most flowers don't do well in this climate. I said something about fruit, and he said he noticed that the mangoes here were unripe. He even said they were white inside. Later on, something about mangoes was niggling at me but I couldn't think what it was."

"I'm still not sure where you're going with this, Sibyl," Mr Buttons said.

"Don't you see? Those mangoes looked ripe enough on the outside, didn't they?"

"Yes, they did," Mr Buttons said.

"And the only opened one was the one shoved in Bradley's mouth. To put it in a nutshell, if anyone looked at that box of mangoes, they would think all those mangoes were ripe. It was only the one in Bradley's mouth that was clearly unripe."

283

Cressida gasped. "So Dennis must be the killer?"

"Unless he saw mangoes in town somewhere," Mr Buttons said.

"I love mangoes," I said. "If any mangoes ever turned up at the supermarket, I'd be the first to know. However, I know it's far too early in the season for mangoes. There's no way any mangoes would be for sale in Little Tatterford, or in Pharmidale, for that matter. It's going to be weeks before any mangoes come to town. Chef Dubois told me he got a box cheaply from a fruit supplier that does the Brisbane to Melbourne run. He hadn't bought any mangoes before that, and he said he certainly won't buy any more until they're in season, so how did Dennis know that the mangoes were a white-green colour inside?"

"Because he smashed one into Bradley's mouth?" Cressida asked me.

I nodded solemnly. "Exactly."

"But that evidence would hardly stand up in a court of law," Mr Buttons said, tapping his chin.

I thought about it for a moment. "Maybe not, but it will give the detectives something to go on. I'm sure they haven't even considered Dennis as a suspect, but once I tell them that, they certainly will."

"Yes, that's a good idea," Mr Buttons said. "Sibyl, call Blake now and tell him, and then call the detectives."

Cressida spoke up. "Sibyl, don't tell Blake about you-know-who."

It took me a moment or two to realise she meant Bertha. I nodded as I pulled the phone out of my pocket to call Blake.

The next thing I knew, someone pushed me hard from behind. I fell against a sturdy, marble topped burr walnut credenza. "I'll take that," a voice said.

I turned around to see Dennis standing in the doorway. "Do as I say and no one will get hurt. Sibyl, hand me your phone."

I handed him my phone with my uninjured arm. Mr Buttons and Cressida were clinging to each other, their faces ashen.

"And don't try to scream," he said. "We're the only ones at the boarding house at the moment."

"So you murdered Bradley Brown!" I said in shock.

He shook his head. "Don't sound so surprised, Sibyl. I heard you talking it all through. What I want to know is, who is this you-know-who that you're not supposed to tell Blake about. I assume it's Bradley's offsider."

"Why didn't you turn Bradley in for the reward?" I asked him. "There must be a reward for the missing money." I was hoping to draw his attention away from trying to find out about Bertha.

"The money he ended up giving me was three times more than the reward," Dennis said. "That will set me up for life, and I can disappear readily enough. I made some good contacts over the years, doing favours for some of the criminal elite in this country. I'll be able to disappear to a nice little country that isn't on good terms with Australia."

"But if he already gave you the money, why did you kill him?" I asked him. "Did you want all the money?"

"All the money would have been nice," he admitted, "but no. He was a loose end. He could have talked at any point, and I knew he had either a best buddy or a girlfriend around who was hiding the money for him. I figured he hadn't told them who I was, but that was only a matter of time."

Mr Buttons finally found his voice. "What made you think he hadn't told his friend who you were?"

Dennis smiled smugly. "I've dealt with criminals for years. I know how they think. They always try to keep people out of the loop to keep them out of danger. I figured I only had a few days left. I was also worried that the interfering fool, Wendy Mason, was here. She could have been a fly in the ointment. I had to act fast."

"When Bradley came into the dining hall that day, he was shocked to see you sitting at the table. I didn't know which one of the boarders he was shocked to see at the time," I added, "but it was obviously you. Since you were in town anyway blackmailing him, why was he so surprised to see you here?"

Dennis worked a crick out of his neck. It made me think of the Terminator, and I shuddered. "He had already given me the money a week previously, and I assured him I was leaving the country at once. When he saw me, he must have realised that I wasn't here for any good reason."

"He thought you were here to murder him," I supplied.

Dennis shrugged. "Actually, he probably thought I was here for more money. Now, enough of this. I need the name of the other person."

"How would we know?" Cressida said in a small voice.

"Because I overheard you say not to tell the police about you-know-who. Now you need to tell me who this you-know-who is, or someone's going to get hurt." His face changed from neutral to violent in an instant.

He lunged for me and grabbed me by the throat, spinning me around to face Mr Buttons and Cressida. "I have no compunction in strangling her with my bare hands if you don't tell me the identity of this person," he snapped.

I could see spots before my eyes. The door flew open. Through the spots I could see a figure, a figure that looked like Chef Dubois. He pulled a knife out of his chef's belt.

Dennis motioned him inside with his free hand. "Drop the knife or she gets it," he said, "and don't get any ideas. I can strangle her before you reach me."

It all happened so fast. I saw the chef raise his arm, and the next thing I knew, I was released. Simultaneously, Dennis let out a scream of pain. I turned around and saw a large knife sticking out of his leg. While I was processing that information, I noticed that he had two knives sticking out of his shoulders. Soon, he was a veritable pincushion.

Mr Buttons lunged for my mobile phone, abandoned on a nearby chair. He called emergency. Cressida ran over to me. "Oh my goodness gracious me, Sibyl. Are you hurt?"

"My throat hurts," I managed to croak.

"I called emergency and then I called Blake for you," Mr Buttons said.

I groaned. This wasn't going to go over well with Blake.

20

We were sitting in my cottage, trying to relax after the events of that afternoon. I was sitting on the sofa next to Blake, who had his arm around me protectively. Sandy was asleep in front of the fire, snoring lightly. Mr Buttons and Cressida were sitting opposite me on separate chairs, as was Albert Dubois. I still didn't know his real name.

Unfortunately, Max was also sitting with us, and acting quite perky for a bird that should soon be asleep on his perch. For some reason, he had taken a liking to Albert and had not insulted him once. That had to be some kind of a record. The rest of us had not got off so lightly. "You're an ugly old fool," Max squawked at Mr Buttons.

"That's it!" I removed Blake's arm from my shoulder and stood up. "I'm putting you outside."

By way of response, Max let out a string of words that could not be repeated. When I returned to the room, I sighed happily. "Apart from the victim, Bradley Brown, no one else was hurt, and that's entirely thanks to you, Albert."

Albert ducked his head, clearly pleased. "Where did you learn to throw knives as well as that?" Mr Buttons asked him. "That was most impressive."

"Oh, I've never thrown a knife before," Albert announced happily. "I'm a darts champion, that's all."

"But you missed my leg by that much," I said, holding my finger and thumb apart about a centimetre.

"Beginner's luck," he said, smiling and nodding.

I thought about the knife that narrowly missed my head, and forced myself to take a deep breath. Blake's arm tightened around my shoulders. "The mystery of the whereabouts of Bradley's money died with him," Blake said.

Cressida, Mr Buttons, and I exchanged glances. We had decided not to tell him about Bertha, or of course, that the other gang members' families had received their share. Who said there is no honour among thieves?

"Dennis took a sizeable cut of it," I said, shuddering when I mentioned his name. "And to think he looked like a nice, honest man."

"Appearances can be deceptive," Mr Buttons said.

Cressida waved her finger at him. "Yes, and I thought you were a nice, normal English gentleman."

Mr Buttons picked up the poker and rearranged the wood on the fire. "I *am* a nice, normal English gentleman," he protested.

"No, you're not!" Cressida said triumphantly. "You're the Fifteenth Earl of Nithwell!"

Mr Buttons turned back to face us. "I'm not, not anymore. I am simply Mr Buttons."

"Why did you leave it all behind you, Mr Buttons?" Albert asked him.

Mr Buttons exhaled loudly. "I wanted to get away from all the unlimited money, the people waiting on my every need, the silver service, the tailored clothes, the people preparing all my meals." He threw up his hands in horror.

I pulled a face. "Well, when you put it like that, it certainly sounds awful." I laughed.

"Things always seem greener on the other side of the fence," Mr Buttons remarked sagely.

"You haven't told me yet why Dennis attacked you all," Blake said. "I know you gave your statement to the detectives, but they didn't tell me and none of you have, either."

"He overheard us wondering who it could be," Mr Buttons said.

Blake shook his finger at all of us. "See? Didn't I tell you investigating could be dangerous?"

"It wasn't investigating as such," I said, crossing my fingers behind my back. "It's just that Dennis happened to remark the other day that the mangoes in town were unripe and white-green inside, and then it dawned on me that the only mangoes in town would have been the ones that you bought, Albert. The only way Dennis would have seen that mango was if he had been the one to stuff it in Bradley's mouth."

Mr Buttons nodded. "And while we knew that wasn't evidence as such," Mr Buttons said, "we were still about to call you."

Cressida chimed in. "Yes Blake, we were about to call you when Dennis came in and tried to strangle Sibyl."

Blake's arm tightened around me. I knew he was about to say something, so I changed the subject. "In all this fuss, I forgot to tell you all that my lawyer called earlier today. My settlement is through. He said it will be in my bank account in a couple of days."

Cressida's face fell. "Does that mean you're going to move out of here and buy a house in town?"

I didn't know what to say. I thought for a moment, and then said, "I like being close to you and Mr Buttons, and while I do love this little cottage, it *is* cramped and tiny. Plus it isn't well insulated." I thought I should stop there to avoid insulting Cressida.

"So you want to go back to living in civilisation?" Mr Buttons asked me.

"Of course not, Mr Buttons," Cressida said in a scolding tone. "Sibyl wants to stay here in Little Tatterford. Isn't that right, Sibyl?"

"Yes, I'm staying in Little Tatterford, and I'd like to stay near you and Mr Buttons, only there are no houses near the boarding house."

Cressida clapped her hands together. "This cottage sits on five acres. Why don't you buy it from me, Sibyl? I could do you a good price, and there are plenty of lovely level home sites on the acreage. Then you'd be just as close to us as you are now. You could build a really big house, big enough for more than just one person." She looked pointedly at Blake as she said it.

My cheeks flushed hot.

"We should talk about this later," Blake said. "I, for one, think it's a great idea. If you *are* going to build a bigger house,"—he winked as he said it—"then perhaps another person should contribute half and it should be bought in joint names."

I fell silent as the implication of his words sank in. Mr Buttons and Cressida beamed widely.

I snuggled against Blake, enjoying the comfortable crackling and woodsy scent of the fire, and looked at my friends, including my new friend Albert, the non-French chef. Several hours ago, things had looked dire. Yet now, they looked the very opposite. I was happy, and filled with hope for the future.

Tequila Mockingbird

When the Fifth Earl of Mockingbird comes to Little Tatterford, all Mr. Buttons' fears come home to roost. And in a cheep shot, when a victim's tequila is poisoned, Mr Buttons becomes the prime suspect. This is where Sibyl and Cressida draw the lime. They fly in the face of the evidence and ruffle a few feathers in an attempt to prove his innocence.

Will the murderer triumph by fowl means?

Or will Sibyl solve the case and have her fairytail ending?

Tequila Mockingbird is Book 7 in this USA Today Bestselling series, Australian Amateur Sleuth.

ABOUT MORGANA BEST

 USA Today Bestselling author Morgana Best survived a childhood of deadly spiders and venomous snakes in the Australian outback. Morgana Best writes cozy mysteries and enjoys thinking of delightful new ways to murder her victims.

www.morganabest.com

Made in the USA
Middletown, DE
12 February 2023

24717579R00184